New York Times and
Br

"Brenda Jackson writes romance that sizzles
and characters you fall in love with."
—*New York Times* and *USA TODAY* bestselling author
Lori Foster

"Jackson's trademark ability to weave
multiple characters and side stories together
makes shocking truths all the more exciting."
—*Publishers Weekly*

"There is no getting away from the sex appeal and
charm of Jackson's Westmoreland family."
—*RT Book Reviews* on *Feeling the Heat*

"Jackson's characters are wonderful, strong,
colorful and hot enough to burn the pages."
—*RT Book Reviews* on *Westmoreland's Way*

"The kind of sizzling, heart-tugging story
Brenda Jackson is famous for."
—*RT Book Reviews* on *Spencer's Forbidden Passion*

"This is entertainment at its best."
—*RT Book Reviews* on *Star of His Heart*

* * *

The Secret Affair is part of The Westmorelands series:
A family bound by loyalty...and love!
Only from *New York Times* bestselling author
Brenda Jackson and Harlequin Desire!

* * *

If you're on Twitter,
tell us what you think of Harlequin Desire!
#harlequindesire

Dear Reader,

It is hard to believe that *The Secret Affair* is my twenty-eighth Westmoreland novel. Time most certainly flies when you're having fun, and I hope you're getting as much enjoyment out of reading about this dynamic family as I am in writing about them.

Holding center stage is Aidan, identical twin to Adrian from *The Real Thing*. From the very beginning the twins were a challenge to their family, but we've watched them grow up and mature. They now see life differently than they did as teens. But the one thing that holds true is that Aidan is a Westmoreland man who will go after what he wants.

And he wants Jillian Novak.

Jillian was first introduced some books back when her older sister Pamela married Dillon Westmoreland. Pam and Dillon are clueless that a romance has been bubbling under their very noses. And that's Aidan and Jillian's secret. Aidan is ready to publicly claim the woman he loves, but Jill is having some misgivings. Find out how Aidan convinces Jill in the most passionate way that true love can't be hidden forever.

I hope you enjoy this story about Aidan and Jillian.

Happy Reading!

Brenda Jackson

BRENDA JACKSON

THE SECRET AFFAIR

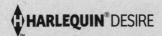 HARLEQUIN® DESIRE

To the man who will always and forever be the love of my life, Gerald Jackson, Sr.

Special thanks to Dr. Dorothy M. Russ of Meharry Medical College for your assistance in providing information on medical schools and residency programs.

In whom are hid all the treasures of wisdom and knowledge.
—*Colossians* 2:3

ISBN-13: 978-0-373-73354-5

Recycling programs for this product may not exist in your area.

The Secret Affair

Printed in U.S.A.

®
™ www.Harlequin.com

BRENDA JACKSON

is a die "heart" romantic who married her childhood sweetheart, Gerald, and still proudly wears the "going steady" ring he gave her when she was fifteen. Their marriage of forty-one years produced two sons, Gerald Jr. and Brandon, of whom Brenda is extremely proud. Because she's always believed in the power of love, Brenda's stories always have happy endings, and she credits Gerald for being her inspiration.

A *New York Times* and *USA TODAY* bestselling author of more than one hundred romance titles, Brenda is a retiree from a major insurance company and now divides her time between family, writing and travel. You may write Brenda at P.O. Box 28267, Jacksonville, Florida 32226, by email at authorbrendajackson@gmail.com or visit her website at www.brendajackson.net.

THE DENVER WESTMORELAND FAMILY TREE

Raphel and Gemma Westmoreland

Stern Westmoreland (Paula Bailey)

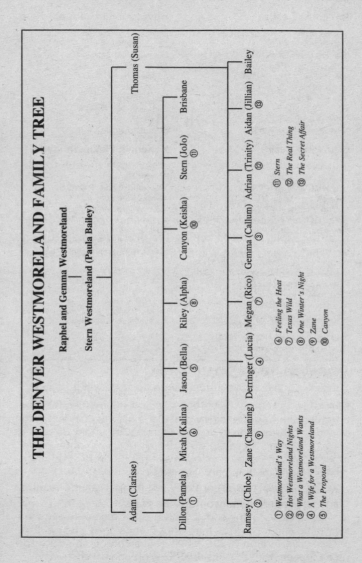

Thomas (Susan)

Adam (Clarisse)

Dillon (Pamela) ①   Micah (Kalina) ⑥   Jason (Bella) ⑤   Riley (Alpha) ⑧   Canyon (Keisha) ⑩   Stern (JoJo) ⑪   Brisbane

Ramsey (Chloe) ②   Zane (Channing) ⑨   Derringer (Lucia) ④   Megan (Rico) ⑦   Gemma (Callum) ③   Adrian (Trinity) ⑫   Aidan (Jillian)   Bailey ⑬

① *Westmoreland's Way*
② *Hot Westmoreland Nights*
③ *What a Westmoreland Wants*
④ *A Wife for a Westmoreland*
⑤ *The Proposal*

⑥ *Feeling the Heat*
⑦ *Texas Wild*
⑧ *One Winter's Night*
⑨ *Zane*
⑩ *Canyon*

⑪ *Stern*
⑫ *The Real Thing*
⑬ *The Secret Affair*

Prologue

Jillian Novak stared across the table at her sister, not believing what she'd just heard.

Jillian placed the glass of wine she'd been holding on the table, barely keeping the drink from spilling. "What do you mean you aren't going with me? That's crazy, Paige. Need I remind you that you're the one who planned the trip?"

"A reminder isn't needed, Jill, but please understand my dilemma," Paige said in a rueful tone, her dark brown eyes shaded with regret. "Getting a part in a Steven Spielberg movie is a dream come true. You can't imagine what I was feeling—happiness at being chosen one minute, and then disappointment the next, when I found out that shooting starts the same week I was supposed to be on the cruise with you."

"Let me guess, your happiness overpowered your disappointment, right?" Jillian felt a pounding pressure in her head and knew why. She had been looking forward to the Mediterranean cruise—for many reasons—and now it appeared she wouldn't be going.

"I'm sorry, Jill. You've never gone on a cruise and I know it's one of the things on your bucket list."

Paige's apology only made Jillian feel worse. She'd

made her sister feel awful for making a choice Jillian would have made herself if given the chance. Reaching across the table, she grabbed Paige's hand.

"I'm the one who should be apologizing, Paige. I was only thinking of myself. You're right. Getting that part in the movie is a dream come true and you'd be crazy not to take it. I'm truly happy for you. Congratulations."

A bright smile spread across Paige's lips. "Thanks. I wanted so much for us to spend time together on the cruise. It's been ages since me, you, Pam and Nadia have had sister time."

Nadia, a senior in college, was their youngest sister. At twenty-one she was two years younger than Paige and four years younger than Jillian. Pamela, their oldest sister—who Jillian, Nadia and Paige were convinced was the best older sister anyone could ever have—was ten years older than Jillian. A former actress, Pam had given up the glitter of Hollywood to return home to Gamble, Wyoming, and raise them when their father died. Now Pam lived in Denver. She was married, the mother of two and the CEO of two acting schools, one in Denver and the other in Gamble. Paige had followed in Pam's footsteps and pursued an acting career. She lived in Los Angeles.

With Pam's busy schedule, she'd said accompanying them on the cruise would have been close to impossible. Nadia had wanted to go but finals kept her from doing so. Jillian had wanted sister time with at least one of her siblings. And now that she had completed medical school, she needed those two weeks on the cruise as a getaway before starting her residency. But there was another reason she wanted to take that two-week cruise.

Aidan Westmoreland.

It was hard to believe it had been a little over a year since she'd broken things off with him. And every time she remembered the reason she'd done so her heart ached. She needed a distraction from her memories.

"You okay, Jill?"

Jillian glanced up at Paige and forced a smile. "Yes, why do you ask?"

"You zoned out on me just now. I was talking and you appeared to be a million miles away. I noticed you haven't been yourself since I arrived in New Orleans. More than once you've seemed preoccupied about something. Is everything okay?"

Jillian waved off Paige's words. The last thing she wanted was for her sister to start worrying and begin digging. "Yes, everything is okay, Paige."

Paige didn't look convinced. "Um, I don't know. Maybe I should forget about being in that movie and go on that cruise with you after all."

Jillian picked up her wineglass to take a sip. "Don't be silly. You're doing the right thing. Besides, I'm not going on the cruise."

"Why not?"

Jillian was surprised at her sister's question. "Surely you don't expect me to go without you."

"You need a break before starting your residency."

Jillian rolled her eyes. "Get real, Paige. What would I do on a two-week cruise by myself?"

"Rest, relax, enjoy the sights, the ocean, the peace and quiet. And you might luck up and meet some nice single guy."

Jillian shook her head. "Nice single guys don't go on cruises alone. Besides, the last thing I need right now is a man in my life."

Paige laughed. "Jill, you haven't had a guy in your life since you dated Cobb Grindstone in your senior year at Gamble High. I think what's missing in your life is a man."

Jillian bristled at her sister's words. "Not hardly, especially with my busy schedule. And I don't see you with anyone special."

"At least I've been dating over the years. You haven't. Or, if you have, you haven't told me about it."

Jillian schooled her expression into an impassive facade. She'd never told Paige about her affair with Aidan, and considering how it had ended she was glad she hadn't.

"Jill?"

She glanced up at her sister. "Yes?"

A teasing smile spread across Paige's lips. "You aren't keeping secrets, are you?"

Jill knew Paige had given her the perfect opportunity to come clean about her affair with Aidan, but she wasn't ready. Even after a year, the pain was still raw. And the last thing Jillian needed was for Paige to start probing for more information.

"You know the reason I don't have a man in my life is because of time. My focus has been on becoming a doctor and nothing else." Paige didn't have to know that a few years ago Aidan had wiggled his way past that focus without much effort. That had been a mistake that cost her.

"That's why I think you should go on that cruise without me," Paige said. "You've worked hard and need to rest and enjoy yourself for a change. Once you begin your residency you'll have even less time for yourself—or anything else."

"That's true," Jillian said. "But—"

"No buts, Jillian."

Jillian knew that tone. She also knew that whenever Paige called her by her full name she meant business. "If I were to go on that cruise alone I'd be bored stiff. You're talking about two weeks."

Paige gave her a pointed look. "I'm talking about two weeks that I believe you need. And just think of all the fabulous places you'll get to see—Barcelona, France, Rome, Greece and Turkey." Now it was Paige who reached out to take hold of Jillian's hand. "Look, Jill, there *is* something going on with you, I can feel it. Whatever it is, it's tearing you apart. I picked up on it months ago, the last time I came to visit you."

A wry smile touched Paige's lips when she added, "Perhaps you *are* keeping secrets. Maybe there's some doctor in medical school that caught your eye and you're not ready to tell me about him. One who has blown your mind and you don't know how to handle the intensity of such a relationship. If that's the case, I understand. All of us at some time or another have issues we prefer to deal with alone. That's why I believe two weeks on the open seas will be good for you."

Jillian drew in a deep breath. Paige didn't know how close she was to the truth. Her problem *did* center on some doctor, but not one attending medical school with her.

At that moment the waitress returned with their meal, and Jillian appreciated the interruption. She knew Paige would not be happy until Jillian agreed to go on the cruise. She'd heard what Paige had said—Paige knew something was bothering Jillian. It would only be a matter of time before Pam and Nadia knew as well, if they didn't already. Besides, Jillian had already taken those two weeks off. If she didn't go on the cruise, the family would expect her to come home and spend that time with them. She couldn't do that. What if Aidan came home unexpectedly while she was there? He was the last person she wanted to see.

"Jill?"

Jillian drew in another deep breath and met Paige's gaze. "Okay, I'll do it. I'll go cruising alone. Hopefully, I'll enjoy myself."

Paige smiled. "You will. There will be plenty for you to do and on those days when you feel like doing nothing, you can do that, too. Everybody needs to give their mind a rest once in a while."

Jillian nodded. Her mind definitely needed a rest. She would be the first to admit that she had missed Aidan—the steamy hot text messages, the emails that made her adrenaline surge and the late-night phone calls that sent heat sizzling through her entire body.

But that had been before she'd learned the truth. Now all she wanted to do was get over him.

She sighed deeply while thinking that Paige was right. Jillian needed that cruise and the time away it would give her. She would go on the cruise alone.

Dr. Aidan Westmoreland entered his apartment and removed his lab coat. After running a frustrated hand down his face, he glanced at his watch. He'd hoped he would have heard something by now. What if…

The ringing of his cell phone made him pause on his way to the kitchen. It was the call he'd been waiting for. "Paige?"

"Yes, it's me."

"Is she still going?" he asked, not wasting time with chitchat.

There was a slight pause on the other end and in that short space of time knots formed in his stomach. "Yes, she's still going on the cruise, Aidan."

He released the breath he'd been holding as Paige continued, "Jill still has no idea I'm aware that the two of you had an affair."

Aidan hadn't known Paige knew the truth, either, until she'd paid him a surprise visit last month. According to her, she'd figured things out the year Jillian had entered medical school. She'd become suspicious when he'd come home for his cousin Riley's wedding and she'd overheard him call Jillian *Jilly* in an intimate tone. Paige had been concerned this past year when she'd noticed Jillian seemed troubled by something that she wouldn't share with Paige.

Paige had talked to Ivy, Jillian's best friend, who'd also been concerned about Jillian. Ivy had shared everything about the situation with Paige. That prompted Paige to fly to Charlotte and confront him. Until then, he'd been clueless as to the real reason behind his and Jillian's breakup.

When Paige had told him of the cruise she and Jillian had planned and had suggested an idea for getting Jillian on the cruise alone, he'd readily embraced the plan.

I've done my part and the rest is up to you, Aidan. I hope you can convince Jill of the truth.

Moments later he ended the call and continued to the kitchen where he grabbed a beer. Popping the top, he leaned against the counter and took a huge gulp. Two weeks on the open seas with Jillian would be interesting. But he intended to make it more than just interesting. He aimed to make it productive.

A determined smile spread across his lips. By the time the cruise ended there would be no doubt in Jillian's mind that he was the only man for her.

Moments later, he tossed the empty can in the recycle bin before heading for the shower. As he undressed, he couldn't help but recall how his secret affair with Jillian had begun nearly four years ago....

One

"So, how does it feel to be twenty-one?"

Jillian's breath caught in her throat when Aidan Westmoreland's tall frame slid into the seat across from her. It was only then that she noticed everyone had gone inside. She and Aidan were the only ones on the patio that overlooked a beautiful lake.

This birthday party had been a huge surprise and Aidan's attendance even more so since he rarely came home from medical school. She couldn't imagine he'd come home just for her birthday. With her away at college most of the time as well, their paths rarely crossed. She couldn't recall them ever holding what she considered a real conversation during the four years she'd known him.

"It feels the same as yesterday," she said. "Age is just a number. No big deal."

A smile touched the corners of his lips and her stomach clenched. He had a gorgeous smile, one that complemented the rest of him. If there was such a thing as eye candy he was certainly it. She had the hots for him big-time.

Who wouldn't have the hots while sitting across from

this hunk of sexiness? If his lips didn't grab you then his eyes certainly would. They were deep, dark and penetrating. Jillian's heart missed beats just looking into them.

"Just a number?" He chuckled, leaning back in his chair, stretching long legs in front of him. "Women might think that way but men think differently."

He smelled good. When did she start noticing the scent of a man?

"And why is that, Aidan?" she asked, picking up her glass of lemonade to take a sip. It suddenly felt hotter than usual. It had nothing to do with the temperature and everything to do with her body's heated reaction to him.

She watched him lift a brow over those striking dark eyes. A feral smile edged his lips as he leaned forward. "Are you sure I'm Aidan and not Adrian?"

Oh, yes she was sure he was Aidan. She'd heard about the games he and his identical twin would play on unsuspecting souls, those who couldn't tell them apart. "I'm sure."

It was Aidan and not Adrian who stirred her in places she'd rather not think about at the moment.

He leaned in even closer. So close she could see the pupils in his dark eyes. "And how are you so certain?" he asked.

Was she imagining things or had the tone of his voice dropped to a husky murmur? It was rumored that he was a big flirt. She had seen him in action at several Westmoreland weddings. It was also a fact that he and his twin were womanizers and had developed quite a reputation at Harvard. She could certainly see why women were at their beck and call.

"Because I am," she replied. And that's all she intended to say on the matter.

There was no way she would tell him the real reason, that from the moment her brother-in-law Dillon had introduced her to Aidan, before he'd married Pam, she had developed a full-blown crush. She'd been seventeen at the time, a senior in high school. The only problem was the crush hadn't lessened much since.

"Why?"

She glanced back up at Aidan. "Why what?"

"Why are you so certain? You still haven't said."

She inwardly sighed. Why couldn't he leave it alone? She had no intention of telling him. But since she had a feeling he wouldn't let up, she added, "The two of you sound different."

He flashed another sexy smile, showing the dimples in his cheeks. Her hormones, which always acted out of control around him, were erratic now. "Funny you say that. Most people think we sound a lot alike."

"Well, I don't think that."

There was no way she could think that when it was Aidan's voice, and not Adrian's, that stroked her senses. Deciding it was time to take charge of the conversation to keep his questions at bay, she inquired, "So how is medical school going?"

He didn't let on that he suspected her ploy, and as she took another sip of her lemonade, he began telling her what she had to look forward to in another year or so. Becoming a neurosurgeon had been a lifelong dream of hers ever since her mother died of a brain infection when Jillian was seven.

Aidan told her about the dual residency program at hospitals in Portland, Maine, and Charlotte, North Carolina, that he planned to pursue after completing medical school. His dream was to become a cardiologist. He was excited about becoming a doctor and she could hear it in his voice. She was thrilled about becoming a doctor one day as well, but she had another year left before she finished her studies at the University of Wyoming.

While he talked, she nodded as she discreetly gave him a slow, appreciative appraisal. The man was too handsome for words. His voice was smooth as silk, with just enough huskiness to keep her pulse rate on edge. Creamy caramel skin spread across the bridge of a hawkish nose, sharp cheekbones, a perfect sculptured jaw and a mouth so sensual she enjoyed watching it in motion. She could imagine all the things he did with that mouth.

"Have you decided where you're going for medical school, Jillian?"

She blinked. He had asked her a question and was waiting on an answer. And while he waited she saw that sexy mouth ease into another smile. She wondered if he'd known she was checking him out.

"I've always wanted to live in New Orleans so working at a hospital there will be at the top of my list," she said, trying to ignore the eyes staring at her.

"And your second choice?"

She shrugged. "Not sure. I guess one in Florida."

"Why?"

She frowned. Why was he quizzing her? "I've never been to Florida."

He chuckled. "I hope that's not the only reason."

Her frown deepened. "Of course that's not the only reason," she said defensively. "There are good medical schools in Louisiana and Florida."

He nodded. "Yes, there are. How's your grade point average?"

"Good. In fact my GPA is better than good. I'm at the top of my class. In the top ten at least."

Getting there hadn't been easy. She'd made a lot of sacrifices, especially in her social life. She couldn't recall the last time she'd gone out on a date or participated in any school activities. But she was okay with that. Pam was paying a lot of the cost for her education and Jillian wanted to make her sister proud.

"What about the entrance exam—the MCAT—and admission essays? Started on them yet?"

"Too early."

"It's never too early. I suggest you prepare for them during your free time."

Now it was her turn to smile. "Free time? What's that?"

The chuckle that erupted from his throat was smooth and sexy and made her pulse thump. "It's time you should squeeze in regardless of whether you think you can or not. It's essential to know how to manage your time wisely, otherwise you'll get burned-out before you even get started."

She grudgingly wondered what made him an expert. Then she pushed her resentment aside. He *was* giving her sound advice and he had gone where she had yet to go. And from what she'd heard, he was doing pretty well at it. He would graduate from Harvard Medical School at the top of his class and then enter a dual residency program that any medical student would die for. He would get the chance to work with the best cardiologists in the United States.

"Thanks for the advice, Aidan."

"You're welcome. When you get ready to knock them out of the way, let me know. I'll help you."

"You will?"

"Sure. Even if I have to come to you to do it."

She lifted a brow. *He would come to her?* She couldn't imagine him doing such a thing. Harvard was in Boston and that was a long way from her university in Laramie, Wyoming.

"Hand me your phone for a second."

His request jarred her thoughts back into focus. "Why?"

"So I can put my numbers into it."

Jillian drew in a deep breath before standing to pull her cell phone from the back pocket of her jeans. She handed it to him and tried to ignore the tingling sensation that flowed through her when their hands touched. She watched him use deft fingers to key in the numbers. Surgeon's fingers. Long, strong, with precise and swift movements. She wondered how those same fingers would feel stroking her skin. She heated just thinking about it.

Moments later his phone rang, interrupting her thoughts. It was then that she realized he'd called himself to have her number, as well. "There," he said, handing her phone back to her. "You now have my number and I have yours."

Was she jumping to conclusions or did his words hold some significance? "Yes, we have each other's numbers," she agreed softly, shoving the assumption out of her mind.

He stood, glancing at his watch. "Adrian and I are meeting up with Canyon and Stern in town for drinks and to shoot pool, so I best get going. Happy birthday again."

"Thanks, Aidan."

"You're welcome."

He walked away but when he got to the French doors he turned and looked back at her, regarding her through his gorgeous dark eyes. The intensity of his gaze made her stomach quiver and another burst of heat swept through her. She felt something...passion? Sexual chemistry? Lust? All three and more, she decided. She'd thought all the Westmoreland males she'd met since Pam married Dillon were eye candy, but there was something about Aidan that pulled at everything female inside of her.

She cleared her throat. "Is anything wrong?" she asked when the silence began to stretch.

Her question seemed to jar him. He frowned slightly before quickly forcing a smile. "Not sure."

As he opened the French door to go inside, she wondered what he meant by that.

Why, of all the women in the world, have I developed this deep attraction for Jillian Novak?

The first time he'd noticed it was when they'd been introduced four years ago. He'd been twenty-two, and she only seventeen, but still a looker. He'd known then that he would have to keep his distance. Now she was twenty-one and still had the word innocent written all over her. From what he'd heard, she didn't even have a boyfriend, preferring to concentrate on her studies and forgo a love life.

And speaking of life, Aidan was fairly certain he loved every part of his, especially his family. So why was he allowing himself to be attracted to Pam's sister? He didn't want to cause any trouble for Dillon.

Pam Novak was a jewel and just what Dillon needed. Everyone had been shocked when Dillon announced he had met a woman who he intended to marry. That had been the craziest thing Aidan had ever heard.

Dillon, of all people, should have known better. Hadn't his first wife left him when he'd refused to send the youngest four members of the Westmoreland family—namely him, Adrian, Bane and Bailey—to foster care? What had made Dillon think Pam would be different? But it didn't take Aidan, his siblings and cousins long to discover that she *was* different.

As far as Aidan was concerned, she was everything they'd *all* needed; she knew the value of family. And she had proven it when she'd turned her back on a promising acting career to care for her three teenaged sisters when her father passed away.

To say the Westmorelands had undergone a lot of family turmoil of their own was an understatement. It all started when Aidan's parents and uncle and aunt died in a plane crash, leaving his cousin Dillon in charge of the family, along with Aidan's oldest brother, Ramsey, as backup. Dillon and Ramsey had worked hard and made sacrifices to keep the family together—all fifteen of them.

Aidan's parents had had eight children: five boys—Ramsey, Zane, Derringer and the twins, Aidan and Adrian—and three girls—Megan, Gemma and Bailey. Uncle Adam and Aunt Clarisse had had seven sons: Dillon, Micah, Jason, Riley, Canyon, Stern and Brisbane.

It hadn't been easy, especially since he, Adrian, Brisbane and Bailey had been under the age of sixteen. And Aidan would admit the four of them had been the most challenging of the bunch, getting into all sorts of mischief, even to the point that the State of Colorado ordered they be put in foster homes. Dillon had appealed that decision and won. Lucky for the four youngest Westmorelands, Dillon had known their acts of rebellion were their way of handling the grief of losing their parents. Now Aidan was in medical school; Adrian was working on his PhD in engineering; Bane had joined the navy and Bailey was taking classes at a local university while working part-time.

Aidan's thoughts shifted back to Jillian, although he didn't want them to. The birthday party yesterday had been a surprise, and the shocked look on her face had been priceless—adorable and a total turn-on. If he'd had any doubt about just how much he was attracted to her, that doubt had been dispelled when he saw her.

She had walked out onto the patio expecting a going-away party for his sister Gemma, who had married Callum and was moving to Australia. Instead it had been a surprise birthday party for her. After shedding a few happy tears, which he would have loved to lick away, she had hugged Pam and Dillon for thinking of her on her twenty-first birthday. From what he'd heard, it was the first time Jillian had had a party since she was a little kid.

While everyone had rushed over to congratulate her, he had hung back, checking her out. The sundress looked cute on her and it was obvious she wasn't the seventeen-year-old he'd met four years ago. Her face was fuller, her features stunning and her body…

Where had those curves come from? There's no way he would have missed them before. She was short compared with his six-foot-two-inch height. He figured she stood no taller than five feet three inches in bare feet. And speaking of her feet, her polished toes, a flaming red, had been another turn on. Pam might not want to hear it, but her sister was Hot with a capital *H*.

When he realized he had been the only one who hadn't wished her a happy birthday, he was about to do so when his phone rang. He had slipped off the patio to take the call from a friend from college who was trying to fix him up on a blind date for next weekend.

When he returned to the patio after finishing his call, everyone else had gone inside to watch a movie or play cards, and she'd been alone. She would never know how hard it had been for him to sit across from her without touching her. She looked good and smelled good, as well.

Jillian Novak had definitely caught his eye.

But Dillon and Pam would pluck out that same eye if he didn't squash what he was feeling.

Everybody knew how protective Pam was when it came to her sisters. Just like everyone knew Aidan wasn't one to take women seriously. And he didn't plan to change his behavior now. So the best thing for him to do while he was home for the next three days was to keep his distance from Jillian as he'd always done.

So why did I get her phone number and give her mine, for crying out loud?

Okay, he reasoned quickly, it had been a crazy moment, one he now regretted. The good thing was he doubted she would ever call him for help and he would make it a point never to call her.

That was a good plan, one he intended to stick to. Now, if he could only stop thinking about her that would be great. Glancing down at the medical journal he was supposed to be reading, he tried to focus on the words. Within a few minutes he'd read one interesting article and was about to start on another.

"Will you do me a *big* favor?"

Aidan glanced up to stare into the face of his sister Bailey. She used to be the baby in the Denver Westmoreland family but that had changed now that Dillon and Pam had a son, and Aidan's brother Ramsey and his wife, Chloe, had a daughter.

"Depends on what the favor is?"

"I promised Jill that I would go riding with her and show her the section of Westmoreland Country that she hasn't seen yet. Now they've called me to come in to work. I need you to go with Jillian instead."

"Just show her another day," he said, quickly deciding that going horseback riding with Jillian wasn't a smart idea.

"That was my original plan but I can't reach her on her cell phone. We were to meet at Gemma Lake, and you know how bad phone reception is out there. She's already there waiting for me."

He frowned. "Can't you ask someone else?"

"I did but everyone is busy."

His frown deepened. "And I'm not?"

Bailey rolled her eyes. "Not like everyone else. You're just reading a magazine."

He figured there was no use explaining to Bailey that his reading was important. He just so happened to be reading about a medical breakthrough where the use of bionic eyes had been tested as a way to restore sight with good results.

"Well, will you do it?"

He closed the medical journal and placed it aside. "You're positive there's no one else who can do it?"

"Yes, and she really wants to see it. This is her home now and—"

"Her home? She's away at school most of the time," he said.

"And so are you, Adrian, Stern and Canyon, and this is still your home. So what's your point?"

He decided not to argue with her. There were times when his baby sister could read him like an open book and he didn't want her to do that in this instance. It wouldn't take her long to figure out the story written on his pages was all about Jillian.

"Fine. I'll go."

"Act a little enthused, will you? You've been kind of standoffish with Jillian and her sisters since Dillon married Pam."

"I have not."

"You have, too. You should take time to get to know them. They're part of the family now. Besides, you and Jill will both become doctors one day so already you have a common interest."

He hoped like hell that would remain their only common interest. It was up to him to make sure it did. "Whatever," he said, standing and walking toward the door, pausing to grab his Stetson off the hat rack.

"And Aidan?"

He stopped before opening the door and turned around, somewhat annoyed. "What now?"

"Try to be nice. You can act like a grizzly bear at times."

That was her opinion. Deciding not to disagree with her, because you could never win with Bailey, he walked out of the house.

Two

Jillian heard the sound of a rider approaching and turned around, using her hand to shield her eyes from the glare of the sun. Although she couldn't make out the identity of the rider, she knew it wasn't Bailey.

The rider came closer and when her heart began pounding hard in her chest, she knew it was Aidan. What was he doing here? And where was Bailey?

Over breakfast she and Bailey had agreed to go riding after lunch. Because the property was located so far from Denver's city limits and encompassed so much land, the locals referred to it as Westmoreland Country. Although Jillian had seen parts of it, she had yet to see all of it and Bailey had volunteered to show it to her.

Dropping her hand to her side, Jillian drew in a deep breath as Aidan and his horse came closer. She tried not to notice how straight he sat in the saddle or how good he looked sitting astride the horse. And she tried not to gawk at how his Stetson, along with his western shirt, vest, jeans and boots, made him look like a cowboy in the flesh.

When he brought the horse to a stop a few feet from where she stood, she had to tilt her head all the way back to look up at him. "Aidan."

He nodded. "Jillian."

His irritated expression and the cutting sound of his voice made her think he was upset about something. Was she trespassing on a particular part of Westmoreland land where she had no business being?

Thinking she needed to give him an explanation, she said, "I'm waiting for Bailey. We're going riding."

"Yes, those *were* your plans."

She lifted a brow. "Were?"

He nodded. "Bailey tried reaching you but your phone is out of range. She was called in to work and asked that I take her place."

"Take her place?"

"Yes, take her place. She indicated you wanted to tour Westmoreland Country."

"I did, but…"

Penetrating dark eyes held hers. "But what?"

She shoved both hands into the pockets of her jeans. There was no way she could tell him that under no circumstances would she go riding anywhere with him. She could barely be around him for a few minutes without becoming unglued…like she was becoming now.

The reason she had placed her hands in her pockets was because they were already sweaty. And then there was that little ball of fire in her stomach that always seemed to burst into flames whenever he was around. Aidan Westmoreland oozed so much sexiness it was driving her to the edge of madness.

"Jillian?"

She blinked when he said her name. The sound of his voice was like a caress across her skin. "Yes?"

"But what? Do you have a problem with me being Bailey's replacement?"

She drew in a deep breath. She couldn't see him being anyone's replacement. It was easy to see he was his own man, and what a man he was. Even now, the weight of his penetrating gaze caused a heated rush to cross her flesh. So, yes, she had a problem with him being Bailey's replacement, but that was something she definitely wouldn't tell him.

"No, I don't have a problem with it," she lied without even blinking. "However, I would think that you do. I'm sure you have more to do with your time than spend it with me."

He shrugged massive shoulders. "No, in fact I don't, so it's not a problem. Besides, it's time for us to get to know each other better."

Why was her body tingling with awareness at his words? She was sure he didn't mean them the way they sounded, but she thought it best to seek clarification. "Why should we get to know each other better?"

He leaned back in the saddle and she couldn't help noticing the long fingers that held the reins. Why was she imagining those same fingers doing things to her, like stroking her hair, splaying up and down her arms, working their way across her naked body? She tried to downplay the shiver that passed through her.

"Dillon married Pam four years ago, and there's still a lot I don't know about you and your sisters," he said, bringing an end to her fantasizing. "We're all family and the Westmorelands are big on family. I haven't been home to get to know you, Paige and Nadia."

With him naming her sisters his earlier statement felt less personal. It wasn't just about her. She should be grateful for that but for some reason she wasn't. "Because of school I haven't been home much, either, but we can get to know each other another time. It doesn't have to be today," she said.

She doubted she could handle his closeness. Even the masculine scent of him was overpowering.

"Today is just as good a day as any. I'm leaving to go back to Boston tomorrow. There's no telling when our paths will cross again. Probably not until we come home for Christmas or something. We might as well do it now and get it over with."

Why did she get the feeling that getting to know her was something he felt forced to do? She took offense at that. "Don't do me any favors," she all but snapped at him while feeling her pulse pound.

"Excuse me?" He seemed surprised by her remark.

"There's no need to get *anything* over with. It's obvious Bailey roped you into doing something you really don't want to do. I can see the rest of Westmoreland Country on my own," she said, untying her horse and then mounting it.

When she sat astride the mare she glanced back over at him. "I don't need your company, Aidan."

He crossed his arms over his chest and she could tell by the sudden tensing of his jaw that he hadn't liked her comment. She was proven right when he said, with a degree of smoldering intensity that she felt through her clothes, "I hate to tell you this, Jillian Novak, but you have my company whether you want it or not."

Aidan stared hard into Jillian's eyes and couldn't help but feel they were waging a battle. Of what he wasn't sure. Of wills? Of desire? Passion? Lust? He rubbed his hand down his face. He preferred none of those things but he had a feeling all of them were fighting for the number one spot right now.

He all but saw steam coming from her ears and figured Jillian didn't like being ordered around.

"Look," he said. "We're wasting time. You want to see the land and I have nothing better to do. I apologize if I came across a little gruff earlier, but by no means did I want to insinuate that I am being forced into showing you around or getting to know you."

There was no need to tell her that Bailey had asked him to be nice to Jillian and her sisters. He'd always been cordial and as far as he was concerned that was good enough. Getting too close to Jillian wasn't a good idea. But then, he was the one who had suggested she call him if she needed help preparing for medical school. He now saw that offer had been a mistake. A big one.

She studied him for a moment and he felt something deep in his gut. It was a lot stronger than the kick in his groin he'd experienced when he'd watched her swing her leg over the back of the horse to mount it. He'd taken a long, explosive breath while fighting the sexual hunger that had roared to life inside of him. Even now, with those beautiful full lips of hers frowning at him, a smoldering spike of heat consumed him. One way he knew he could put a stop to this madness was to get her out of his system, since she seemed to have gotten under his skin.

But the way he would do that wasn't an option...not if he loved his life.

"You're sure about this?"

Hell no, he wasn't sure about anything concerning her. Maybe the main reason behind his attraction to her, in addition to her striking beauty, was that he truly didn't know her that well. Maybe once he got to know her he'd discover that he didn't like her after all.

"Yes, I'm sure about this, so come on," he said, nudging his horse forward to stand beside hers. "There's a lot to see so I hope you're a fairly good rider."

She gave him a smile that made him appreciate the fullness of her mouth even more. "Yes, I'm a fairly good rider."

And then she took off, easing her horse into a canter. He watched in admiration as she flawlessly jumped the horse over a flowing creek.

He chuckled to himself. She wasn't a fairly good rider; she was an excellent one.

Jillian slowed her pace and glanced over her shoulder to see Aidan make the same jump she had. She couldn't help but be impressed at his skill, but she shouldn't be surprised. She'd heard from Dillon that all his brothers and cousins were excellent horsemen.

In no time, he'd caught up with her. "You're good," he said, bringing his horse alongside hers. The two animals eased into a communal trot.

"Thanks," she said, smiling over at him. "You're not bad yourself."

He threw his head back and laughed. The robust sound not only floated across the countryside, but it floated across her, as well. Although she'd seen him smile before, she'd never seen him amused about anything.

"No, I'm not bad myself. In fact there was a time I wanted to be a bronco rider in the rodeo."

For some reason she wasn't surprised. "Dillon talked you out of it?"

He shook his head, grinning. "No, he wouldn't have

done such a thing. One of Dillon's major rules has been for us to choose our own life goals. At least that was his rule for everyone but Bane."

She'd heard all about Aidan's cousin Brisbane Westmoreland, whom everyone called Bane. She'd also heard Dillon had encouraged his baby brother to join the military. He'd said Bane could do that or possibly go to prison for the trouble he'd caused. Bane had chosen the navy. In the four years that Pam had been married to Dillon, Jillian had only seen Bane twice.

"So what changed your mind about the rodeo?" she asked when they slowed the horses to a walk.

"My brother Derringer. He did the rodeo circuit for a couple of summers after high school. Then he got busted up pretty bad. Scared all of us to death and I freaked out. We all did. The thought of losing another family member brought me to my senses and I knew I couldn't put my family through that."

She nodded. She knew about him losing his parents and his aunt and uncle in a plane crash, leaving Dillon—the oldest at the time—to care for all of them. "Derringer and a few of your cousins and brothers own a horse-training business right?"

"Yes and it's doing well. They weren't cut out to work in the family business so after a few years they left to pursue their dreams of working with horses. I try to help them out whenever I come home but they're doing a great job without me. Several of their horses have won important derbies."

"Ramsey resigned as one of the CEOs as well, right?" she asked of his oldest brother.

He glanced over at her. "Yes. Ramsey has a degree in agriculture and economics. He'd always wanted to be a sheep farmer, but when my parents, aunt and uncle died in that plane crash he knew Dillon would need help at Blue Ridge."

Jillian knew that Blue Ridge Land Management was a Fortune 500 company Aidan's father and uncle had started years ago. "But eventually he was able to pursue his dream, right?"

Aidan nodded. "Yes. Once Dillon convinced Ramsey he could handle things at the corporation without him. Ramsey's sheep ranch is doing great."

She nodded. She liked Ramsey. In fact, she liked all the Westmorelands she had gotten to know. When Pam married Dillon, the family had welcomed her and her sisters with open arms. She'd discovered some of them were more outgoing than the others. But the one thing she couldn't help but notice was that they stuck together like glue.

"So how did you learn to ride so well?" he asked.

"My dad. He was the greatest and although I'm sure he wanted at least one son, he ended up with four girls. He felt we should know how to do certain things and handling a horse was one of them," she said, remembering the time she'd spent with her father and how wonderful it had been for her.

"He evidently saw potential in me because he made sacrifices and sent me to riding school. I competed nationally until he got sick. We needed the money to pay for his medicine and doctor bills."

"Do you regret giving it up?" he asked.

She shook her head. "No. I enjoyed it but making sure Dad got the best care meant more to me...more to all of us...than anything." And she meant it. There had been no regrets for any of them about giving up what they'd loved to help their father.

"Here we are."

She looked around at the beauty of the land surrounding her, as far as her eyes could see and beyond. Since Dillon was the oldest, he had inherited the main house along with the three hundred acres it sat on. Everyone else, upon reaching the age of twenty-five, received one hundred acres to call their own. Some parts of this area were cleared and other parts were dense with thick foliage. But what took her breath away was the beautiful waterway that branched off into a huge lake. Gemma Lake. She'd heard it had been named after Aidan's great-grandmother.

"This place is beautiful. Where are we exactly?"

He glanced over at her and smiled. "My land. Aidan's Haven.

Aidan's Haven, she immediately decided, suited him. She could see him building his home on this piece of land one day near this huge waterway. Today he looked like a cowboy, but she could see him transforming into a boat captain.

"Aidan's Haven. That's a nice name. How did you come up with it?"

"I didn't. Bailey did. She came up with all the names for our one-hundred-acre plots. She chose names like Stern's Stronghold, Zane's Hideout, Derringer's Dungeon, Ramsey's Web and Megan's Meadows, just to name a few."

Jillian had visited each of those areas and all the homes that had been built on the land were gorgeous. Some were single-story ranch-style designs, while others were like mansions with several floors. "When do you plan to build?"

"Not for a while yet. After medical school I'll probably work and live somewhere else for a while since I have six years of residency to complete for the cardiology program."

"But this will eventually be your home."

A pensive look appeared on his face. "Yes, Westmoreland Country will always be my home."

She'd always thought she would live in Gamble, Wyoming. Although she knew she would leave for college, she figured she would return one day and work in the hospital there before setting up a practice of her own. After all, she had lived there her entire life; all her friends were there. But after Pam married Dillon things changed for her, Paige and Nadia. They were close to their oldest sister and decided to leave Wyoming and make their homes close to Pam's. It had worked out well for everyone. Nadia was in her last year of high school here in Colorado and Paige was in California attending UCLA.

"What about you? Do you ever plan to return to Gamble, Wyoming, to live, Jillian?"

Again, she wondered why her stomach tightened whenever he said her name. Probably had something to do with that deep, husky voice of his.

"No, I don't plan to return to Gamble. In fact, Nadia and Paige and I talked a few weeks ago and we plan to approach Pam about selling the place. She would have done so already, but she thinks we want to keep it as part of our legacy."

"You don't?"

"Only because we've moved on and think of Denver

as home now. At least Nadia and I do. Paige has made a life for herself in Los Angeles. She's hoping her acting career takes off. We're hoping the same thing for her. Pam has done so much for us already and we don't want her to feel obligated to pay more of our college tuition and expenses, especially when we can use the money from the sale of the house to do so."

He nodded. "Let's take a walk. I want to show you around before we move on to Adrian's Cove."

He dismounted and tied his horse to a nearby tree. Then he turned to help her down. The moment he touched her, awareness of him filled her every pore. From the look in his eyes it was obvious that something similar was happening to him.

This was all new to her. She'd never felt anything like this before. And although her little lovemaking session with Cobb Grindstone on prom night had appeased her curiosity, it had left a lot to be desired.

As soon as her feet touched the ground, she heard a deep moan come from Aidan's throat. Only then did it become obvious that they'd gotten caught up in a carnal attraction that was so sharp it took her breath away.

"Jillian…"

He said her name again and, like all the other times, the deep, husky sound accentuated his sexiness. But before she could respond, the masculine hand planted around her waist nudged her closer and then his mouth lowered to hers.

Three

All sorts of feelings ripped through Aidan, making him totally conscious of the woman whose lips were locked to his. Deep in the center of his being he felt a throb unlike any he'd ever felt before—an intense flare of heat shooting straight to his loins.

He knew he had to stop. This wasn't any woman. This was Jillian Novak, Pam's sister. Dillon's sister-in-law. A woman who was now a part of the Westmoreland family. All that was well and good, but at the moment the only thing his mind could comprehend was that she had desire clawing at his insides and filling his every cell with awareness.

Instead of yielding to common sense, he was captivated by her sweet scent and her incredible taste, and the way her tongue stroked his showed both boldness and innocence. She felt exquisite in his arms, as if she belonged there. He wanted more. He wanted to feel her all over, kiss her all over. Taste her. Tempt her with sinful enticements.

The need for air was the only reason he released her lips, but her flavor made him want to return his mouth to hers and continue what they'd started.

The shocked look in her eyes told him she needed time to comprehend what had just happened between them. She took a step back and he watched as she took a deep breath.

"We should not have done that."

Aidan couldn't believe she had the nerve to say that while sultry heat still radiated off her. He might have thought the same thing seconds ago, but he couldn't agree with her now. Not when his fingers itched to reach out and pull her back into his arms so he could plow her mouth with another kiss. Dammit, why did her pouty lips look so inviting?

"Then why did we do it?" he countered. He might have made the first move but she had definitely been a willing participant. Her response couldn't lie. She had enjoyed the kiss as much as he had.

"I don't know why we did it, but we can't do it again."

That was easy for her to say. "Why not?"

She frowned at him. "You know why not. Your cousin is married to my sister."

"And?"

She placed her hands on her hips giving him a mind-boggling view of her slim waist line. "And we can't do it again. I know all about your womanizing reputation, Aidan."

Her words struck a nerve. "Do you?"

"Yes. And I'm not interested. The only thing I'm interested in is getting into medical school. That's the only thing on my mind."

"And the only thing on mine is getting out of medical school," he countered in a curt tone. "As far as Dillon being married to Pam, it changes nothing. You're still a beautiful woman and I'm a man who happens to notice such things. But since I know how the situation stands between us, I'll make sure it doesn't happen again."

"Thank you."

"You're welcome. Glad we got that cleared up. Now I can continue showing you around."

"I'm not sure that's a good idea."

He watched her and when she pushed a lock of hair away from her face, he again thought how strikingly beautiful she was. "Why not? You don't think you can control yourself around me?" he asked, actually smiling at the possibility of that being true.

Her look of anger should have warned him, but he'd never been one to heed signs. "Trust me, that's definitely not it."

"Then there's no reason for me not to finish showing you around, is there, Jillian? Besides, Bailey will give me hell about it if I don't. There's a lot of land we still have to cover so let's get started."

He began walking along the bank of the river and figured that after cooling off Jillian would eventually catch up.

Jillian watched Aidan walk ahead and decided to hang back a moment to reclaim her common sense. Why had she allowed him to kiss her? And why had she enjoyed it so much?

The man gave French kissing a whole new definition, and she wasn't sure her mouth would ever be the same.

No one had ever kissed her like that before. No one would have dared. To be honest, she doubted anyone she'd ever kissed would know how. Definitely not Cobb. Or that guy in her freshman year at Wyoming University, Les, that she'd dropped really quickly when he wanted to take her to a hotel and spend the night on their first date. He might have been a star on the school's football team, but from the couple of times they had kissed, compared to what she'd just experienced with Aidan, Les had definitely dropped the ball.

But then, regardless of how enjoyable Aidan's kiss had been, she was right in what she'd told him about not repeating it. She had no business getting involved with a guy whose favorite sport was messing around. She knew better. Honestly, she didn't know what had come over her.

However, she knew full well what had come over him. More than once she'd overheard Dillon express his concern to Pam that although the twins were doing well at Harvard, he doubted they would ever settle down into serious relationships since they seemed to enjoy being womanizers. That meant Aidan's interest in her was only because of overactive testosterone. Pam had warned Jillian numerous times about men who would mean her no good, and her oldest sister would be highly disappointed if Jillian fell for the ploy of a man like Aidan. A man who could take away her focus on becoming a doctor just to make her his plaything.

Feeling confident she had her common sense back on track, she began walking. Aidan wasn't too far ahead and it wouldn't take long for her to catch up with him. In the meantime she couldn't help but appreciate his manly physique. His faded jeans emphasized masculine thighs, a rock-solid behind, tight waist and wide shoulders. He didn't just walk, he swaggered, and he did it so blatantly sexily, it increased her heart rate with every step he took.

Moments later he slowed and turned around to stare at her, pinning her with his dark gaze. Had he felt her ogling him? Did he know she had been checking out his rear big-time? She hoped not because his front was just as impressive. She could see why he was in such high demand when it came to women.

"You coming?"

I will be if you don't stop looking at me like that, Jillian thought, getting closer to where he stood. She felt the heat of his gaze on every inch of her. She came to a stop in front of him. She couldn't take looking into his eyes any longer so she glanced around. In addition to the huge lake there were also mountains surrounding the property. "You have a nice mountain view in this spot and can see the lake from here," she said.

"I know. That's why I plan to build my house right here."

She nodded. "Have you designed it yet?"

"No. I don't plan on building for several more years, but I often come here and think about the time when I will. The house will be large enough for me and my family."

She snapped her head around. "You plan on getting married?"

His chuckle was soft but potent. "Yes, one day. That surprises you?"

She decided to be honest. "Yes. You do have a reputation."

He leaned one broad shoulder against a Siberian elm tree. "This is the second time today that you've mentioned something about my reputation. Just what have you heard about me?"

She took a seat across from him on a huge tree stump. "I heard what hellions you, Adrian, Bailey and Bane used to be."

He nodded solemnly. "Yes, we were that. But that was a long time ago, and I can honestly say we regretted our actions. When we grew older and realized the impact we'd had on the family, we apologized to each one of them."

"I'm sure they understood. You were just children and there was a reason you did what you did," she said. She'd heard the full story from Pam. The deaths of their parents, and aunt and uncle, had been the hardest on those youngest four. Everyone had known that their acts of rebellion were their way of handling their grief.

"Sorry I mentioned it," she said, feeling bad that she'd even brought it up.

He shrugged. "No harm done. It is what it is. It seems the four of us got a reputation we've been trying to live down for years. But I'm sure that's not the reputation of mine that you were really referring to."

No, it wasn't. "I understand you like women."

He chuckled. "Most men do."

She raised a brow, not in the least amused. "I mean you really like them, but you don't care about their feelings. You break their hearts without any concern for the pain it might cause."

He studied her for a long moment. "That's what you heard?"

"Yes. And now you want me to believe that you're seriously considering settling down one day, marrying and having a family?"

"Yes. One doesn't have anything to do with the other. What I do now in no way affects any future plans. I need to clarify something. I don't deliberately set out to break any woman's heart. I tell any woman I date the truth up front—my career as a doctor is foremost. However, if she refuses to take me at my word and assumes that she can change my mind, then it's not my fault when she finds out otherwise."

"So in other words…"

"In other words, Jillian, I don't intentionally set up any woman for heartbreak or lead her on," he answered curtly.

She knew she should probably leave well enough alone and stop digging, but for some reason she couldn't help herself. "However, you do admit to dating a *lot* of women."

"Yes, I admit it. And why not? I'm single and don't plan to get into a committed relationship anytime soon. And contrary to what you believe, I don't date as many women as you might think. My time is pretty limited these days because of medical school."

She could imagine. How he managed to date at all while in medical school was beyond her. He was definitely into multitasking. She'd discovered most relationships demanded a lot of work and it was work she didn't have time for. Evidently he made things easy by not getting serious with any woman. At least he'd been honest about it. He dated women for the fun of it and didn't love any of them.

"I have one other question for you, Aidan," she said, after drawing in a deep breath.

"What's your question?"

"If all of what you said is true, about not getting serious with any woman, then why did you kiss me?"

Now that was a good question, one he could answer but really didn't want to. She did deserve an answer, though, especially after the way he had plowed her mouth earlier. She was twenty-one, five years younger than him. And although she'd held her own during their kiss, he knew they were worlds apart when it came to sexual experience. Therefore, before he answered her, he needed to ask a few questions of his own.

"Why did you kiss me back?"

He could tell by her expression that she was surprised by his counterquestion. And, as he'd expected, she tried to avoid giving him an answer. "That's not the issue here."

He couldn't help but smile. Little did she know it *was* the issue, but he would touch on that later. "The reason I kissed you, Jillian, is because I was curious. I think you have a beautiful pair of lips and I wanted to taste them. I wanted to taste you. It's something I've wanted to do for a while."

He saw her jaw drop and had to hold his mouth closed for a second to keep from grinning. She hadn't expected him to answer her question so bluntly or to be so direct. That's something she needed to know about him. He didn't sugarcoat anything. *Straightforward* could be his middle name.

"So now that you know my reason for kissing you, what was your reason for kissing me back?"

She began nibbling on her bottom lip. Watching her made him ache, made him want to take hold of those lips and have his way with them again.

"I—I was…"

When she didn't say anything else, he lifted a brow. "You were what?"

Then she had the nerve to take her tongue and lick those same lips she'd been nibbling on moments ago. "I was curious about you, too."

He smiled. Now they were getting somewhere. "I can

understand that. I guess the reason you asked about the kiss is because I told you I'm not into serious relationships when it comes to women. I hope you don't think a deep kiss constitutes a serious relationship."

From the look on her face, which she quickly wiped off, that's exactly what she'd thought. She was more inexperienced than he'd assumed. He wondered just how inexperienced she was. Most twenty-one-year-old women he knew wore desire, instead of their hearts, on their sleeves.

"Of course I knew that."

If she knew that then why were they having this conversation? If she thought he was looking for something serious just because he'd kissed her then she was so far off the mark it wasn't funny.

"How many boyfriends have you had?"

"Excuse me?"

No, he wouldn't excuse her. There were certain things she needed to know. Things experience had nothing to do with. "I asked how many boyfriends you've had. And before you tell me it's none of my business, I'm asking for a reason."

She lifted her chin in a defiant pose. "I can't imagine what reason you would have for needing to know that."

"So you can protect yourself." He thought she looked both adorable and sexy. From the way her curly hair tumbled down her shoulders to the way the smoothness of her skin shone in the sunlight.

She lifted a brow. "Against men like you?"

"No. Men like me would never mislead you into thinking there was anything serious about a kiss. But there are men who would lead you to think otherwise."

She frowned. "And you don't think I can handle myself?"

He smiled. "Not the way I think you should. For some reason you believe you can avoid kisses until you're in a serious relationship and there are certain kisses that can't be avoided."

He could tell by her expression that she didn't believe him. "Take the kiss we shared earlier. Do you honestly think you could have avoided it once I got started?" he asked her.

Her frown deepened. "Yes, of course I could have."

"Then why didn't you?"

She rolled her eyes. "I told you. The only reason I allowed you to kiss me, and the only reason I participated, is because I was curious."

"Really?"

She rolled her eyes again. "Really. Truly."

"So, you're not curious anymore?"

She shook her head. "Nope, not at all. I wondered what kissing you was like and now I know."

Deciding to prove her wrong and settle the matter once and for all, he moved away from the tree and walked toward her.

Figuring out his intent, she stood with a scowl on her face. "Hold it right there, Aidan Westmoreland. Don't you dare think you're going to kiss me again."

When he reached her, he came to a stop directly in front of her and she refused to back up. Instead she stood her ground. He couldn't help but admire her spunk, although in this case it would be wasted.

"I do dare because I don't just think it, Jillian, I know it. And I also know that you're going to kiss me back. *Again.*"

Four

Jillian doubted she'd ever met a more arrogant man. And what was even worse, he had the nerve to stand in front of her with his Stetson tipped back and his legs braced apart in an overconfident stance. How dare he tell her what she would do? Kiss him back? Did he really believe that? Honestly?

She tilted her head back to glare up at him. He didn't glare back, but he held her gaze in a way that was unnerving. And then his eyes moved, slowly raking over her from head to toe. Was that desire she felt rushing through her body? Where had these emotions inside of her come from? Was she getting turned on from the way he was looking at her? She tried to stiffen at the thought but instead she was drawn even more into the heat of his gaze.

"Stop that!"

He lifted a brow. "Stop what?"

"Whatever you're doing."

He crossed his arms over his chest. "So, you think I'm responsible for the sound of your breathing? For the way your nipples have hardened and are pressing against your shirt? And for the way the tip of your tongue is tingling, eager to connect with mine?"

Every single thing he'd pointed out was actually happening to her, but she refused to admit any of them. She crossed her arms over her own chest. "I have no idea what you're talking about."

"Then I guess we're at a standoff."

"No, we're not," she said, dropping her hands to her sides. "I'm leaving. You can play this silly game with someone else."

She turned to go and when his hand reached out and touched her arm, sharp spikes of blood rushed through her veins, filling her pores, drenching the air she was breathing with heated desire. And what on earth was that hunger throbbing inside of her at the juncture of her thighs? And what were those slow circles he was making on her arm with his index finger? She expelled a long deep breath and fought hard to retain control of her senses.

Jillian wanted to snatch her arm away but found she couldn't. What kind of spell had he cast on her? Every hormone in her body sizzled, hissed and surged with a need she'd never felt before. She couldn't deny the yearning pulsing through her even if she wanted to.

"You feel it, don't you, Jillian? It's crazy, I know, and it's something I can't explain, but I feel it each and every time I'm within a few feet of you. As far as I'm concerned, Pam and Dillon are the least of our worries. Figuring out just what the hell is going on between us should be at the top of the agenda. You can deny it as long as you want, but that won't help. You need to admit it like I have."

She did feel it and a part of her knew there was real danger in admitting such a thing. But another part knew he was right. With some things it was best to admit there was a problem and deal with it. Otherwise, she would lay awake tonight and regret not doing so.

His hand slowly traveled up her arm toward her lips. There he cradled her mouth in the palm of his hands. "And whatever it is has me wanting to taste you and has you wanting to taste me. It has me wanting to lick your mouth dry and you wanting to lick mine in the same way."

He paused a moment and when he released a frustrated breath she knew that whatever this "thing" was between them, he had tried fighting it, as well. But he had given up the fight and was now ready to move to the next level, whatever that was.

"I need to taste you, Jillian," he said.

As much as she wished otherwise, there was a deep craving inside of her to taste him, too. Just one more time. Then she would walk away, mount her horse and ride off like the devil himself was after her. But for now she needed this kiss as much as she needed to breathe.

She saw him lowering his head and she was poised for the exact moment when their mouths would connect. She even parted her lips in anticipation. His mouth was moving. He was whispering something but instead of focusing on what he was saying, her gaze was glued to the erotic movement of his lips. And the moment his mouth touched hers she knew she had no intention of turning back.

Nothing could have prepared Aidan for the pleasure that radiated through his body. How could she arouse him like no other woman could? Instead of getting bogged down in the mystery of it all, he buried his fingers in her hair, holding her in place while his mouth mated hungrily with hers.

And she was following his lead, using her tongue with the same intensity and hunger as he was using his. It was all about tasting, and they were tasting each other with a greed that had every part of his body on fire.

He felt it, was in awe of it. In every pore, in every nerve ending and deep in his pulse, he felt it. Lowering his hand from her hair he gently gripped her around the waist and, with their mouths still locked, he slowly maneuvered her backward toward the tree he'd leaned against earlier. When her back rested against the trunk, her thighs parted and he eased between them, loving the feel of his denim rubbing against hers.

Frissons of fire, hotter than he'd ever encountered, burned a path up his spine and he deepened the kiss as if his life depended on him doing so. Too soon, in his estimation, they had to come up for air and he released her mouth just as quickly as he'd taken it.

He tried not to notice the thoroughly kissed look on her face when she drew in a deep breath. He took a step back so he wouldn't be tempted to kiss her again. The next time he knew he wouldn't stop with a kiss. He wouldn't be satisfied until he had tasted her in other places, as well. And then he would want to make love to her, right here on his land. On the very spot he planned to build his house. Crap! Why was he thinking such a thing? In frustration, he rubbed a hand down his face.

"I think we need to move on."

Her words made him look back at her and an ache settled deep in his stomach. She was beautiful and desire escalated through him all over again. Giving in to what he wanted, he took a step forward and lowered his mouth to hers, taking a sweep of her mouth with his tongue. His groin swelled when she caught his tongue and began sucking on it.

He broke off the kiss and drew in a ragged breath. "Jillian! You're asking for trouble. I'm within two seconds of spreading you on the ground and getting inside of you." The vision of such a thing nearly overpowered his senses.

"I told you we should go. You're the one who kissed me again."

He smiled. "And you kissed me back. Now you understand what I meant when I said there are some kisses that can't be avoided. You didn't want me to kiss you initially, but then you did."

She frowned slightly. "You seduced me. You made me want to kiss you."

His smile widened. "Yes, to both."

"So this was some sort of lesson?"

He shook his head. "Not hardly. I told you I wanted to taste you. I enjoyed doing so."

"This can't become a habit, Aidan."

"And I don't intend to make it one, trust me. My curiosity has more than been satisfied."

She nodded. "So has mine. Are you ready to show me the other parts of Westmoreland Country?"

"Yes. We're headed for Adrian's Cove next and then Bailey's Bay and Bane's Ponderosa."

He backed up to give her space and when she moved around him, he was tempted to reach out and pull her back into his arms, kiss her some more, until he got his fill. But he had a feeling that getting his fill would not be possible and that was something he didn't want to acknowledge.

* * *

"So, how did the tour go with Aidan yesterday?"

Jillian glanced up from her breakfast when Bailey slid into the chair next to her. Pam had shared breakfast with Jillian earlier before leaving for the grocery store, and had asked her the same thing. It had been hard to keep a straight face then and it was harder to do so now.

"It went well. There's a lot of land in Westmoreland Country. I even saw the property you own, Bailey's Bay."

Bailey smiled. "I can't claim ownership until I'm twenty-five so I have a couple years left. But when I do, I plan to build the largest house of them all. It will even be bigger than this one."

Jillian thought that would be an accomplishment because Dillon and Pam's house was huge. Their house was three stories and had eight bedrooms, six bathrooms, a spacious eat-in kitchen, a gigantic living room, a large dining room with a table that could seat over forty people easily, and a seven-car-garage.

"I can't wait to see it when you do." Jillian liked Bailey and had from the first time she'd set foot in Westmoreland Country to attend Pam's engagement party. And since there was only a couple years' difference in their ages, with Bailey being older, they had hit it off immediately. "What happens if you meet and marry a guy who wants to take you away from here?"

"That won't happen because there's not a man alive who can do that. This is where I was born and this is where I'll die."

Jillian thought Bailey sounded sure of that. Hadn't Jillian felt the same way about her home in Wyoming at one time? Although it hadn't been a man that had changed her mind, it had been the thought of how much money Pam would be paying for three sisters in college. Although her older sister had married a very wealthy man, it still would not have been right.

"Besides," Bailey said, cutting into her thoughts. "I plan to stay single forever. Having five bossy brothers and seven even bossier male cousins is enough. I don't need another man in my life trying to tell me what to do."

Jillian smiled. When she'd heard the stories about all the trouble Bailey used to get into when she was younger, Jillian had found it hard to believe. Sitting across from her was a beautiful, self-confident woman who seemed to have it going on. A woman who definitely knew what she wanted.

"I hope Aidan was nice and didn't give you any trouble."

Jillian lifted a brow. "Why would you say that?"

Bailey shrugged. "Aidan has his moods sometimes."

"Does he?"

"Yes, but if you didn't pick up on them then I guess he did okay."

No, she hadn't picked up on any mood, but she had picked up on his sensual side. And he had definitely picked up on hers. She was still in a quandary as to exactly what had happened yesterday. It was as if she'd become another person with him. She'd discovered that being kissed senseless wasn't just a cliché but was something that could really happen. Aidan had proven it. Even after brushing her teeth twice, rinsing out her mouth and eating a great breakfast Pam had prepared, the taste of him was still deeply embedded on her tongue. And what was even crazier was that she liked it.

Knowing Bailey was probably expecting a response,

she said. "Yes, he was okay. I thought he was rather nice."

Bailey nodded. "I'm glad. I told him he needed to get to know you and your sisters better since he's rarely home. And we're all family now."

All family now. Bailey's words were a stark reminder of why what happened yesterday could never be repeated. They weren't just a guy and a girl who'd met with no connections. They had deep connections. Family connections. And family members didn't go around kissing each other. Why of all the guys out there did she have to be attracted to one with the last name Westmoreland?

"So, besides Bailey's Bay where else did he take you?"

To heaven and back. The words nearly slid from Jillian's lips because that's where she felt she'd actually been. Transported there and back by a kiss. Amazing. Pulling her thoughts together, she said, "First, we toured Aidan's Haven."

"Isn't it beautiful? That's the property I originally wanted because of the way it's surrounded by Gemma Lake. But then I realized it would have been too much water to deal with. I think the spot where Aidan plans to build his house is perfect, though, and will provide an excellent view of the lake and mountains, no matter what room of the house you're in."

Jillian agreed and eradicated the thought from her mind that Aidan's wife and kids would one day live there. "I also saw Adrian's Cove. That piece of property is beautiful, as well. I love the way it's surrounded by mountains."

"Me, too."

"And from there we visited Bailey's Bay, Canyon's Bluff and Stern's Stronghold."

"Like the names?"

Jillian smiled. "Yes, and I heard they were all your idea."

"Yes," Bailey said, grinning. "Being the baby in the family has its benefits. Including the opportunity to play musical beds and sleep at whatever place I want. I was living with Dillon full-time, but after he married I decided to spread myself around and check out my brothers', sisters' and cousins' abodes. I like driving them crazy, especially when one of my brothers or cousins brings his girlfriend home."

Jillian couldn't help but laugh. Although she wouldn't trade her sisters for the world, it had to be fun having older brothers and male cousins to annoy.

"What's so funny?"

Jillian's heart skipped a beat upon hearing that voice and knowing who it belonged to. Aidan leaned in the kitchen doorway. Wearing a pair of jeans that rode low on his hips and a muscle shirt, he looked too sexy for her peace of mind. She couldn't help studying his features. It was obvious he'd just gotten out of bed. Those dark eyes that were alert and penetrating yesterday had a drowsy look. And she couldn't miss the dark shadow on his chin indicating he hadn't shaved yet. If he looked like that every morning, she would just love to see it.

"I thought you'd already left to return to Boston," Bailey said, getting up and crossing the room to give him a hug. Jillian watched the interaction and a part of her wished she could do the same.

"I won't be leaving until tomorrow."

"Why did you change your plans?" Bailey asked, surprised. "Normally, you're in a rush to get back."

Yes, why? Jillian wondered as well and couldn't wait for his answer.

"Because I wasn't ready to go back just yet. No big deal."

"Um," Bailey said, eyeing her brother suspiciously, "I get the feeling it is a big deal and probably has to do with some woman. I heard you, Adrian and Stern didn't get in until late last night."

Jillian turned her gaze away from Bailey and Aidan and took a sip of her orange juice. The spark of anger she suddenly felt couldn't be jealousy over what Bailey had just said. Had Aidan kissed Jillian senseless, then gone somewhere last night and kissed someone else the same way? Why did the thought of him doing that bother her?

"You ask too many questions, Bay, and stay out my business," Aidan said. "So, what's so funny, Jillian?"

Jillian drew in a deep breath before turning back to Aidan. "Nothing."

Bailey chuckled. "In other words, Aidan, stay out of *her* business."

Jillian heard his masculine grunt before he crossed the room to the coffeepot. The kitchen was huge, so why did it suddenly feel so small now that he'd walked in? And why did he have to walk around with such a sexy saunter?

"Well, I hate to run but I promised Megan that I would house-sit for a few hours so I'm headed for Megan's Meadows. Gemma is decorating the place before leaving for Australia and is sending her crew over to hang new curtains."

Megan and Gemma were Bailey and Aidan's sisters,

whom Jillian liked tremendously. Megan was a doctor of anesthesiology at one of the local hospitals and Gemma was an interior designer who owned Designs by Gem.

Bailey turned to Jillian. "You're here until tomorrow, right?"

"Yes."

"Then maybe Aidan can show you the parts of Westmoreland Country that you missed yesterday."

Jillian could feel Aidan's gaze on her. "I wouldn't want to put him to any trouble."

"No trouble," Aidan said, "I don't have anything else to do today."

Bailey laughed. "Until it's time for you to go and hook up with the woman who's the reason you're staying around an extra day."

"Goodbye, Bay," Aidan said in what Jillian perceived as an annoyed tone.

Bailey glanced over her shoulder at him while departing. "See you later, Aidan. And you better not leave tomorrow before telling me goodbye." She swept out of the kitchen and Jillian found herself alone with Aidan.

She glanced over at him and saw him leaning back against the counter with a cup of coffee in his hand, staring at her.

She drew in a deep breath when Aidan asked, "How soon can we go riding?"

Five

Aidan couldn't help staring into Jillian's eyes. He thought she had the most beautiful eyes of any woman he'd ever seen. And that included all those women who'd thrown themselves at him last night.

"I'm not going anywhere with you, Aidan. Besides, I'm sure the reason you changed your plans to remain in Denver another day has nothing to do with me."

Boy was she wrong. It had everything to do with her. He had spent three hours in a nightclub last night surrounded by beautiful women and all he could think about was the one he considered the most beautiful of all. Her.

A possibility suddenly hit him. Was she jealous? Did she actually believe that crap Bailey had just spouted about him changing his schedule because of some woman? He didn't know whether to be flattered or annoyed that she, or any woman, thought they mattered enough that they should care about his comings and goings. But in all honesty, what really annoyed him was that she *was* beginning to matter. And the reason he had decided to hang in Denver another day was because of her.

Instead of saying anything right away, for fear he might say the wrong thing, he turned and refilled his coffee cup. Then he crossed the room and slid into the chair across from her. Immediately, he sensed her nervousness.

"I don't bite, Jillian," he said, before taking a sip of coffee.

"I hope not."

He couldn't help but smile as he placed his cup down. He reached out and closed his fingers around her wrist. "Trust me. I prefer kissing you to biting you."

She pulled her hand back and nervously glanced over her shoulder before glaring at him. "Are you crazy? Anyone could walk in here!"

"And?"

"And had they heard what you just said they would have gotten the wrong impression."

He leaned back in his chair. "What do you think is the *right* impression?"

Her hair was pulled back in a ponytail and he was tempted to reach out, release the clasp and watch the waves fall to her shoulders. Then he would run his fingers through the thick, black tresses. He could just imagine the light, gentle strokes on her scalp and the thought sent a sudden jolt of sexual need through him.

"I don't want to make any impression, Aidan. Right or wrong."

Neither did he. At least he didn't think he did. Damn, the woman had him thinking crazy. He rubbed a frustrated hand down his face.

"It was just a kiss, nothing more."

He looked over at her. Why was he getting upset that she thought that way when he should be thinking the same thing. Hadn't he told her as much yesterday?

"Glad you think that way," he said, standing. "So let's go riding."

"Didn't you hear what I said?"

He smiled down at her. "You've said a lot. What part in particular are you asking about?"

She rolled her eyes. "I said I'm not going anywhere with you."

His smile widened. "Sure you are. We're going riding because if we don't, Bailey will think it's because I did something awful and got you mad with me. And if she confronts me about it, I will have to confess and tell her the truth—that the reason you wouldn't go riding with me is because you were afraid I might try to kiss you again. A kiss you can't avoid enjoying."

She narrowed her gaze at him. "You wouldn't."

"Trust me, I would. Confessing my sins will clear my conscience but will they clear yours? I'm not sure they would since you seem so wrapped up in not making any right or wrong impressions."

She just sat there and said nothing. He figured she was at a loss for words and this would be the best time for him to leave her to her thoughts. "Let's meet at the same place where we met yesterday in about an hour," he said, walking off to place his cup in the dishwasher.

Before exiting the kitchen he turned back to her and said, "And just so you know, Jillian, the reason I'm not leaving today to return to Boston has nothing to do with some woman I met at the club last night, but it has everything to do with you."

It has everything to do with you.

Not in her wildest dreams had Jillian thought seven little words could have such a huge impact on her. But they did. So much so that an hour later, she was back in the same place she'd been yesterday, waiting on Aidan.

She began pacing. Had she lost her mind? She wasn't sure what kind of game he was playing but instead of putting her foot down and letting him know she wanted no part of his foolishness, somehow she got caught, hook, line and sinker.

And all because of a kiss.

She would have to admit, it had been more than just a kiss. The fact that he was a gorgeous man, a man she'd had a secret crush on for four years, probably had a lot to do with it. But she'd always been able to separate fact from fiction, reality from fantasy, good from bad. So what was wrong with her now? An association with Aidan would only bring on heartache because not only was she deceiving her sister and brother-in-law, and no doubt the entire Westmoreland family, but she was deceiving herself, as well. Why would she want to become involved with a man known as a womanizer?

But then, she really wasn't involved with him. He was taking her riding, probably he would try to steal a few kisses and then nothing. Tomorrow he would return to Boston and she would return to Wyoming and it would be business as usual. But she knew for her it wouldn't be that simple.

She turned when she heard his approach. Their gazes connected and a luscious shiver ran through her body. He rode just like he had yesterday and looked basically the same. But today something was different. Now she knew he had the mouth of a very sensual man. A mouth he definitely knew how to use.

"I was hoping you would be here," he said, bringing his horse to a stop a few feet from her.

"Did you think I wouldn't after what you threatened to do?"

"I guess not," he said, dismounting.

"And you have no remorse?"

He tipped his Stetson back to gaze at her. "I've heard confession is good for the soul."

"And just what would it have accomplished, Aidan?"

"Putting it out there would have cleared your conscience, since it obviously bothers you that someone might discover I'm attracted to you and that you're attracted to me."

She started to deny what he'd said about her being attracted to him, but decided not to waste her time. It was true and they both knew it. "A true gentleman never kisses and tells."

"You're right. A true gentleman doesn't kiss and tell. But I don't like the thought of you cheapening what happened yesterday, either."

She placed her hands on her hips and leaned in, glaring at him. "How is it cheapening it when the whole thing meant nothing to you anyway?"

Jillian's question stunned Aidan. For a moment he couldn't say anything. She had definitely asked a good question, and it was one he wasn't sure he could answer. The only response he could come up with was that the kisses should not have meant anything to him, but they had. Hell, he had spent the past twenty-four hours thinking about nothing else. And hadn't he changed his plans so that he could stay another day just to spend more time with her?

She was standing there, glaring at him, with her arms crossed over her chest in a way that placed emphasis on a nice pair of breasts. Full and perfectly shaped. He could just imagine running his hands over them, teasing the nipples before drawing them in his mouth to...

"Well?"

She wanted an explanation and all he wanted to do was erase the distance separating them, take her into his arms and kiss that glare right off her face. Unfortunately, he knew he wouldn't stop there. Whether she knew it or not, Jillian Novak's taste only made him want more.

"Let's ride," he said, moving toward his horse. Otherwise, he would be tempted to do something he might later regret.

"Ride?" she hissed. "Is that all you've got to say?"

He glanced back over at her as he mounted his horse. "For now."

"None of this makes any sense, Aidan," she said, mounting her own horse.

She was right about that, he thought. None of it made any sense. Why was she like a magnet pulling him in? And why was he letting her?

They had ridden a few moments side by side in total silence when she finally broke it by asking, "Where are we going?"

"Bane's Ponderosa."

She nodded. "Has he built anything on it?"

"No, because legally it's not his yet. He can't claim it until he's twenty-five."

"Like Bailey. She told me about the age requirement."

"Yes, like Bailey."

He wished they could go back to not talking. He needed the silence to figure out what in the hell was happening to him. She must have deciphered that he was not in a talkative mood because she went silent again.

Aidan glanced over at her, admiring how well she handled a horse. He couldn't help admiring other things, as well. Such as how she looked today in her jeans and western shirt, and how the breasts he had fantasized about earlier moved erotically in rhythm with the horse's prance.

"There is a building here," Jillian said, bringing her horse to a stop.

He forced his eyes off her breasts to follow her gaze to the wooden cabin. He brought his horse to a stop, as well. "If you want to call it that, then yes. Bane built it a while back. It became his and Crystal's secret lovers' hideaway."

"Crystal?"

"Yes. Crystal Newsome. Bane's one and only."

Jillian nodded. "She's the reason he had to leave and join the navy, right?"

Aidan shrugged. "I guess you could say that, although I wouldn't place the blame squarely on Crystal's shoulders. Bane was as much into Crystal as Crystal was into Bane. They were both sticks of dynamite waiting to explode."

"Where is she now?"

"Don't know. I'm not sure if Bane even knows. He never says and I prefer not to ask," Aidan said, getting off his horse and tying it to the rail in front of the cabin.

He moved to assist her from her horse and braced himself for the onslaught of emotions he knew he would feel when he did so.

"You don't have to help me down, Aidan. I can manage."

"I'm sure you can but I'm offering my assistance anyway," he said, reaching his arms up to her.

For a minute he thought she would refuse his offer, but then she slid into his embrace. And as expected the moment they touched, fire shot through him. He actually felt his erection throb. He didn't say anything as he stared into her face. How could she arouse him to this degree?

"You can let go of me now, Aidan."

He blinked, realizing her feet were on the ground yet his arms were still around her waist. He tried to drop his arms but couldn't. It was as if they had a mind of their own.

Then, in a surprise move, she reached up and placed her arms around his neck. "This is crazy," she whispered in a quiet tone. "I shouldn't want this but I'm not thinking straight."

He shouldn't want it, either, but at that moment nothing could stop him. "We're leaving tomorrow. When we get back to our respective territories we can think straight then."

"What about right now?" she asked, staring deep into his gaze.

"Right now all I want to do is taste you again, Jillian. So damn bad."

She lifted her chin. "Then do it."

He doubted she knew what she was saying because her lips weren't the only thing he wanted to taste. He lowered his mouth to hers, thinking that she would find that out soon enough.

At that particular moment, Jillian couldn't deny herself the enjoyment of this kiss even if her life had depended on it.

She was getting what she wanted in full force—Aidan Westmoreland–style.

She stood with her arms wrapped around his neck and their lips locked, mesmerized, totally captivated, completely enthralled. How his tongue worked around in her mouth was truly remarkable. Every bone, every pore and every nerve ending responded to the way she was being thoroughly kissed. When had she become capable of such an intense yearning like this, where every lick and suck of Aidan's tongue could send electrical waves through her?

"Let's go inside," he whispered, pulling back from the kiss while tonguing her lips.

"Inside?" She could barely get the question past the feeling of burning from the inside out.

"Yes. We don't need to be out here in the open."

No they didn't. She had gotten so caught up in his kiss that she'd forgotten where they were. But instead of saying they shouldn't even be kissing, in the open or behind closed doors, she didn't resist him when he took her hand and tugged her toward the cabin.

Once the door closed behind them she looked around and was surprised at how tidy the place was. Definitely not what she'd expected. It was a one-room cabin with an iron bed. The colorful bedspread matched the curtains and coordinated with the huge area rug.

She turned to Aidan. "This is nice. Who keeps this place up?"

"Gemma promised Bane that she would and of course she had to put her signature on it. Now that she's getting married and moving to Australia, Bailey will take over. This place is important to Bane. He spends time here whenever he comes home."

Jillian nodded. "How's he doing?"

Aidan shrugged. "Okay now. It was hard for him to buckle down and follow authority, but he has no other choice if he wants to be a SEAL."

She'd heard that was Bane Westmoreland's goal. "So no one usually comes out this way?" She needed to know. There would be no turning back after today and she needed to make sure they didn't get caught.

"Rarely, although Ramsey uses this land on occasion for his sheep. But you don't have to worry about anyone showing up if that's what you're worried about."

She turned to face him. "I don't know why I'm doing this."

He touched her chin and tilted her head back to meet his gaze. "Do you want me to tell you?"

"Think you got it all figured out?"

He nodded. "Yes, I think I do."

"Okay then, let's hear it," she said, backing up to sit on the edge of the bed.

He moved to sit down on a nearby stool. "We're attracted to each other."

She chuckled slightly. "Tell me something I don't know, Aidan."

"What if I say that we've sort of gotten obsessed with each other?"

She frowned. "*Obsessed* is too strong a word, I think. We've only kissed twice."

"Actually three times. And I'm dying for the fourth. Aren't you?"

She knew she had to be honest with him and stop denying the obvious. "Yes, but I don't understand why."

He got up from the stool and stood. "Maybe it's not for us to understand, Jillian."

"How can you say that? How do you think our family would react if they knew we were carrying on like this behind their backs?"

He slowly crossed the room to stand in front of where she sat. "We won't know how they'd react because you're determined to keep this a secret, aren't you?"

She tilted her head to look up at him. "Yes. I couldn't hurt Pam that way. She expects me to stay focused on school. And if I did get involved with a guy, I'm sure she wouldn't want that guy to be you."

He frowned. "And what is so bad about getting involved with me?"

"I think you know the answer to that. She thinks of us as one big family. And there's your reputation. But, like you said, we'll be leaving tomorrow and going our separate ways. What's happening between us is curiosity taking its toll on our common sense."

"That's what you think?" he asked, reaching out and taking a lock of her hair between his fingers.

"Yes, that's what I think." She noticed something in the depths of his eyes that gave her pause—but only for a second. That's all the time it took for her gaze to lower from his eyes to his mouth.

She watched as he swept the tip of his tongue across his lips. "I can still taste you, you know," he said in a low, husky tone.

She nodded slowly. "Yes, I know." Deciding to be honest, she said, "And the reason I know is because I can still taste you, as well."

Six

Aidan wished Jillian hadn't said that. After their first kiss, he'd concluded she had enjoyed it as much as he had. When they'd gone another round he'd been sure of it. Just like he was sure that, although her experience with kissing had been at a minimum, she was a fast learner. She had kept up with him, stroke for stroke. And now, for her to confess that she could still taste him, the same way he could still taste her, sent his testosterone level soaring.

He took a step closer, gently pulled her to her feet and wrapped his arms around her waist. He truly didn't understand why the desire between them was so intense but he accepted that it was. The thought of Dillon and Pam's ire didn't appeal to him any more than it did to her, but unlike her, he refused to believe his cousin and cousin-in-law would be dead set against something developing between him and Jillian.

But he didn't have to worry because *nothing* was developing between them. They were attracted to each other; there was nothing serious about that. He'd been attracted to women before, although never to this degree, he would admit. But after today it would be a while before they saw each other again since he rarely came home. This would be a one-and-done fling. He knew for certain that Pam and Dillon would definitely *not* like the thought of that. They would think he'd taken advantage of her. So he agreed they did not need to know.

"I won't sleep with you, Aidan."

Her words interrupted his thoughts. He met her gaze. "You won't?"

"No. I think we should get that straight right now."

He nodded slowly. "All right. So what did you have in mind for us to do in here?" To say he was anxious to hear her answer was an understatement.

"Kiss some more. A lot more."

Evidently she didn't think an intense kissing match could lead to other things, with a loss of control topping the list. "You think it will be that simple?"

She shrugged. "No. But I figure if we both use a reasonable degree of self-control we'll manage."

A reasonable degree of self control? Jillian had more confidence in their abilities than he did. Just being here with her was causing a hard pounding in his crotch. If only she knew just how enticing she looked standing in front of him in a pair of jeans and a white button-up blouse that he would love to peel off her. Her hair was pinned up on her head, but a few locks…like the one he'd played with earlier…had escaped confinement.

"Is there a problem, Aidan?"

He lifted a brow. "Problem?"

"Yes. You're stalling and I'm ready now."

He fought to hide his grin. Was this the same woman who only yesterday swore they would never kiss again? The same woman who just that morning had refused to go riding with him? Her enthusiasm caused something within him to stir, making it hard to keep his control in check. His body wouldn't cooperate mainly because her scent alone was increasing his desire for her.

And she thought all they would do was some heavy-duty kissing?

Deciding not to keep her waiting any longer, he slanted his mouth over hers.

When had she needed a man's kiss this much? No, *this* much, she thought, leaning up on her toes to become enmeshed in Aidan's kiss even more. Jillian felt his arms move from around her waist to her backside, urging her closer to the fit of him, making her feel his hard erection pressing against her middle. She shouldn't like how it felt but she did.

The tips of her nipples seemed sensitized against his solid chest. When had she become this hot mass of sexual desire?

When he intensified the kiss even more, she actually heard herself moan. Really moan. He was actually tasting her. Using his mouth to absorb hers as if she was a delectable treat he had to consume. She was losing all that control she'd told him they had to keep and she was losing it in a way she couldn't define.

When he groaned deep in his throat and deepened the kiss even more, it took all she had to remain standing and not melt in a puddle on the floor. Why at twenty-one was she just experiencing kisses like these? And why was she allowing her mind to be sacked with emotions and sensations that made it almost impossible to breathe, to think, to do anything but reciprocate? Their tongues tangled greedily, dueling and plowing each other's mouths with a yearning that was unrelenting.

When she noticed his hands were no longer on her

backside but had worked their way to the zipper of her jeans, she gasped and broke off the kiss, only to be swept off her feet into Aidan's strong arms.

Before she could ask what he was doing, he tumbled them both onto the huge bed. She looked up into his dark eyes as he moved his body over hers. Any words she'd wanted to say died in her throat. All she could do was stare at him as intense heat simmered through her veins. He leaned back on his haunches and then in one quick movement, grasped her hips and peeled the jeans down to her knees.

"What—what are you doing?" she managed to ask, while liquid fire sizzled down her spine. She was lying there with only bikini panties covering her.

He met her gaze. "I'm filling my entire mouth with the taste of you." And then he eased her panties down her legs before lifting her hips and lowering his head between her thighs.

The touch of his tongue had her moaning and lifting her hips off the bed. He was relentless, and he used his mouth in a way that should be outlawed. She wanted to push his head away, but instead she used her arms to hold him in place.

And then she felt a series of intense spasms spread through her entire body. Suddenly, he did something wicked with his tongue, driving her wild. She screamed as a flood of sensations claimed her, tossing her into an earth-shaking orgasm. Her very first. It was more powerful than anything she could have imagined.

And he continued to lap her up, not letting go. His actions filled her with more emotions, more wanting, more longing. Her senses were tossed to smithereens. It took a while before she had enough energy to breathe through her lungs to release a slow, steady breath. She wondered if she had enough energy to even mount her horse, much less ride away from here.

Aidan lifted his head and slowly licked his lips, as if savoring her taste, while meeting her eyes. "Mmm, delicious."

His words were as erotic as she felt. "Why? Why did you do that?" she asked, barely able to get the words out. She felt exhausted, totally drained. Yet completely and utterly satisfied.

Instead of giving her an answer, he touched her chin with the tip of his thumb before lowering his lips to hers in an open-mouth kiss that had fire stirring deep in her stomach. Tasting herself on his lips made her quiver.

When he finally released her lips, he eased back on his haunches and gazed down at her. "I did it because you have a flavor that's uniquely you and I wanted to sample it."

She lifted her hips off the bed when he pulled her jeans back up. Then he shifted his body to pull her into his lap. She tilted her head back to look at him. "What about when we leave here tomorrow?"

"When we leave tomorrow we will remember this time with fondness and enjoyment. I'm sure when you wake up in your bed in Wyoming and I wake up in mine in Boston, we will be out of each other's systems."

She nodded. "You think so?"

"Yes, I'm pretty sure of it. And don't feel guilty about anything because we haven't hurt anyone. All we did was appease our curiosity in a very delectable way."

Yes, it had been most delectable. And technically, they hadn't slept together so they hadn't crossed any lines. She pulled away from him to finish fixing her clothing, tucking her shirt back into her jeans.

"Um, a missed opportunity."

She glanced over at him. "What?"

"Your breasts. I had planned to devour them."

At that moment, as if on cue, her breasts began to ache. Her nipples felt tight, sensitive, pulsing. And it didn't help matters when an image of him doing that very thing trickled through her mind.

"We need to go," she said quickly, knowing if they remained any longer it would only lead to trouble.

"Do we?"

He wasn't helping matters by asking her that. "Yes. It's getting late and we might be missed." When he made no attempt to move, she headed for the door. "I can find my way back."

"Wait up, Jillian."

She stopped and turned back to him. "We don't have to go back together, Aidan."

"Yes, we do. Pam knows of our plans to go riding together."

Color drained from Jillian's face. "Who told her?"

"I ran into her when I was headed to the barn and she asked where I was headed. I told her the truth."

At the accusation in her expression, he placed his hands in the back pockets of his jeans. "Had I told her I was going someplace else and she discovered differently, Jillian, she would have wondered why I had lied."

Jillian nodded slowly upon realizing what he said made sense. "What did she say about it?"

"Nothing. In fact I don't think she thought much about it at all. However, she did say she was glad you were about to start medical school and she would appreciate any advice I could give you."

Jillian swallowed tightly. He'd given her more than advice. Thanks to him, she had experienced her first orgasm today. "Okay, we'll ride back together. I'll just wait outside."

She quickly walked out the door. He'd claimed what they'd done today would get them out of each other's systems. She definitely hoped so.

When the door closed behind Jillian, Aidan rubbed a hand down his face in frustration. He couldn't leave Denver soon enough. The best thing to do was put as much distance between him and Jillian as possible. She felt uncomfortable with the situation and now he was beginning to feel the same. However, his uneasiness had nothing to do with Dillon and Pam finding out what they'd been up to, and everything to do with his intense attraction to Jillian.

Even now he wanted to go outside, throw her over his shoulders and bring her back inside. He wanted to kiss her into submission and taste her some more before making nonstop love to her. How crazy was that?

He'd never felt this much desire for any woman, and knowing she was off-limits only seemed to heighten his desire for her. And now that he'd gotten an intimate taste of her, getting her out of his system might not be as easy as he'd claimed earlier. Her taste hadn't just electrified his taste buds, it had done something to him that was unheard of—he was no longer lingering on the edge of wanting to make love to her but had fallen off big-time.

Every time his tongue explored her mouth, his emotions heated up and began smoldering. And when he lapped her up, he was tempted to do other things to her, as well. Things he doubted she was ready for.

Drawing in a deep breath, he straightened up the bed-covers before heading for the door. Upon stepping outside, he breathed in deeply to calm his racing heart. She stood there stroking his horse and a part of him wished she would stroke him the same way. He got hard just imagining such a thing.

He didn't say anything for a long moment. He just stood there watching her. When his erection pressed uncomfortably against his zipper, he finally spoke up. "I'm ready to ride."

She glanced over at him and actually smiled when she said, "You have a beautiful horse, Aidan."

"Thanks," he said, walking down the steps. "Charger is a fourth-generation Westmoreland stallion."

She turned to stroke the horse again and didn't look up when he came to stand next to her. "I've heard all about Charger. I was warned by Dillon to never try to ride him because only a few people could. It's obvious you're one of those people."

Aidan nodded. "Yes, Charger and I have an understanding."

She stopped stroking Charger to look at him. "What about you and me, Aidan? Do we have an understanding?"

He met her gaze, nor sure how he should answer that. Just when he thought he had everything figured out about them, something would happen to make his brains turn to mush. "I assume you're referring to the incidents that have taken place between us over the past two days."

"I am."

"Then, yes, we have an understanding. After today, no more kissing, no more touching—"

"Or tasting," she interjected.

Saying he would never again taste her was a hard one, but for her peace of mind and for his own, he would say it. "Yes, tasting."

"Good. We're in agreement."

He wouldn't exactly say that, but for now he would hold his tongue—that same tongue that enjoyed dueling with hers. "I guess we need to head back."

"Okay, and I don't need your help mounting my horse."

In other words, she didn't want him to touch her. "You sure?"

"Positive."

He nodded and then watched her move away from his horse to get on hers. As usual, it was a total turn-on watching her. "I want to thank you, Aidan."

He took his gaze away from the sight of her legs straddling the horse to look into her face. "Thank me for what?"

"For introducing me to a few things during this visit home."

For some reason that made him smile. "It was my pleasure." And he meant every word.

Seven

"You're still not going home, Jillian?"

Jillian looked up from eating her breakfast to see her roommate, Ivy Rollins. They had met in her sophomore year when Jillian knew she didn't want to live in the dorm any longer. She had wanted an apartment off campus and someone to share the cost with her. Ivy, who had plans to attend law school, had answered the ad Jillian placed in the campus newspaper. They'd hit it off the first time they'd met and had been the best of friends since. Jillian couldn't ask for a better roommate.

"I was home last month," she reminded Ivy.

"Yes, but that was a couple of days for your birthday. Next week is spring break."

Jillian didn't want to be reminded. Pam had called yesterday to see if Jillian would be coming home since Nadia had made plans to do so. Paige, who was attending UCLA, had gotten a small part in a play on campus and needed to remain in Los Angeles. Guilt was still riding Jillian over what she and Aidan had done. She hated deceiving her sister about anything. "I explained to Pam that I need to start studying for the MCAT. She understood."

"I hate leaving you, but—"

"But you will," Jillian said, smiling. "And that's fine. I know how homesick you get." That was an understatement. Ivy's family lived in Oregon. Her parents, both chefs, owned a huge restaurant there. Her two older brothers were chefs as well and assisted her parents. Ivy had decided on a different profession than her parents and siblings, but she loved going home every chance she got to help out.

"Yes, I will," Ivy said, returning her smile. "In fact I leave in two days. Sure you'll be okay?"

"Yes, I'll be fine. I've got enough to keep me busy since I'm sitting for the MCAT in two months. And I need to start working on my essays."

"It's a bummer you'll be doing something other than enjoying yourself next week," Ivy said.

"It's okay. Getting into medical school is the most important thing to me right now."

A few hours later Jillian sat at the computer desk in her bedroom searching the internet. She had tossed around the idea of joining a study group for the MCAT and there appeared to be several. Normally, she preferred studying solo but for some reason she couldn't concentrate. She pushed away from the computer and leaned back in her chair knowing the reason.

Aidan.

It had been a little over a month since she'd gone home for her birthday, and Aidan had been wrong. She hadn't woken up in her bed in Wyoming not thinking of him. In fact she thought of him even more. All the time. Thoughts of him had begun interfering with her studies.

She got up and moved to the kitchen to grab a soda from the refrigerator. He should have been out of her system by now, but he wasn't. Memories of him put her to sleep at night and woke her up in the morning. And then in the wee hours of the night, she recalled in vivid detail his kisses, especially the ones between her legs.

Remembering that particular kiss sent a tingling sensation through her womanly core, which wasn't good. In fact, nothing about what she was going through was good. Sexual withdrawal. And she hadn't even had sex with Aidan, but she hadn't needed sex to get an orgasm. That in itself showed the magnitude of his abilities.

Returning to her bedroom she pushed thoughts of him from her mind. Sitting back down at her desk, she resumed surfing the net. She bet he hadn't even given her a thought. He probably wasn't missing any sleep thinking of her, and he had probably woken up his first day back in Boston with some woman in his bed. Why did that thought bother her?

She had been tempted to ask Pam if she'd heard from Aidan, but hadn't for fear her sister would wonder why Jillian was inquiring about Aidan when she hadn't before.

Jillian turned around when she heard a knock on her bedroom door. "Come in."

Ivy walked into the room, smiling. "I know you have a lot to do but you've been in here long enough. Come grab a bite to eat at the Wild Duck. My treat."

Ivy wasn't playing fair. She knew the Wild Duck was one of Jillian's favorite eating places. They had the best hamburgers and fries. "You've twisted my arm," she said, pushing away from the desk.

Ivy chuckled. "Yeah. Right."

Jillian stood, thinking she did need a break. And maybe she could get Aidan off her mind.

* * *

"How are you doing, Dr. Westmoreland?"

Aidan smiled over at the doctor who'd transferred in to the medical school during the weekend that he'd gone home. He really should ask her out. Lynette Bowes was attractive, she had a nice figure, and she seemed friendly enough. At times almost too friendly. She enjoyed flirting with him and she'd gone so far as to make a few bold innuendos, which meant getting her into his bed probably would be easy. So what was he waiting on?

"I'm fine, Dr. Bowes, and how are you?"

She leaned over to hand him a patient's chart, intentionally brushing her breasts against his arm. "I would be a lot a better if you dropped by my apartment tonight," she whispered.

Another invite. Why was he stalling? Why wasn't he on top of his game as usual? And why was he thinking that the intimate caress she'd purposely initiated just now had nothing on the caresses he'd experienced with Jillian?

"Thanks, but I have plans for tonight," he lied.

"Then maybe another night?"

"I'll let you know." He appreciated his cell phone going off at that moment. "I'll see you later." He made a quick escape.

Later that night while at home doing nothing but flipping TV channels, he couldn't help wondering what the hell was wrong with him. Although he'd asked himself that question, he knew the answer without thinking.

Jillian.

He'd assumed once he was back in Boston and waking up in his own bed that he would eradicate her from his mind. Unfortunately, he'd found out that wasn't the case. He thought about her every free moment, and he even went to bed thinking about her. And the dreams he had of her were double X-rated. His desire for her was so bad that he hadn't thought twice about wanting anyone else.

And it hadn't helped matters when he'd called home earlier in the week and Dillon mentioned that Jillian wasn't coming home for spring break. She told Pam she had registered to take the MCAT and needed the time to study and work on her admissions essays. He applauded her decision to make sacrifices to reach her goal, but he was disappointed she hadn't reached out to him liked he'd suggested. He'd made a pretty high score on the MCAT and could give her some study pointers. He'd even keyed his contact information into her phone.

Yet she hadn't called to ask him a single question about anything. That could only mean she didn't want his help and had probably pushed what happened between them to the back of her mind. Good for her, but he didn't like the fact that she remained in the center of his.

Tossing the remote aside he reached for his cell phone to pull up her number. When her name appeared he put the phone down. They'd had an agreement, so to speak. An understanding. They would put that time in Denver behind them. It had been enjoyable but was something that could not and would not be repeated. No more kissing, touching...or tasting.

Hell, evidently that was easy for her to do, but it was proving to be downright difficult for him. There were nights he woke up wanting her with a passion, hungering to kiss her, touch her and taste her.

The memories of them going riding together, especially that day spent in Bane's cabin...every moment of that time was etched in Aidan's mind, making his brain cells overload.

Like now.

When he'd pulled down her jeans, followed by her panties, and had buried his head between her legs and tasted her…the memory made his groin tighten. Need for Jillian clawed at him in a way that made it difficult to breathe.

Aidan stood and began pacing the floor in his apartment, trying to wear down his erection. He paused when an idea entered his mind. He had time he could take off and he might as well do it now. He'd only been to Laramie, Wyoming, a couple of times, and maybe he should visit there again. He would take in the sights and check out a few good restaurants. And there was no reason for him not to drop in on Jillian to see how she was doing while he was there.

No reason at all.

Three days later, Jillian sat at the kitchen table staring at the huge study guide in front of her. It had to be at least five hundred pages thick and filled with information to prepare her for the MCAT. The recommendation was that students take three months to study, but since she was enrolled in only one class this semester she figured she would have more time to cram and could get it done in two months. That meant she needed to stay focused. No exceptions. And she meant none.

But her mind was not in agreement, especially when she could lick her lips and imagine Aidan doing that very same thing. And why—after one month, nine days and twenty minutes—could she still do that? Why hadn't she been able to forget about his kisses and move on? Especially now when she needed to focus.

The apartment was empty and felt lonely without Ivy. It was quiet and just what she needed to get some serious studying done. She had eaten a nice breakfast and had taken a walk outside to get her brain and body stimulated. But now her mind wanted to remember another type of stimulation. One that even now sent tingles through her lower stomach.

She was about to take a sip of her coffee when the doorbell sounded. She frowned. Most of her neighbors were college students like her, and the majority of them had gone home for spring break. She'd noticed how vacant the parking lot had looked while out walking earlier.

Getting up from the kitchen table she moved toward the front door. She glanced through her peephole and her breath caught. Standing on the other side of her door was the one man she'd been trying not to think about.

Shocked to the core, she quickly removed the security chain and unlocked the door. Opening it, she tried to ignore the way her heart pounded and how her stomach muscles trembled. "Aidan? What are you doing here?"

Instead of answering, he leaned down and kissed her. Another shock rammed right into the first. She should have pushed him away the moment their mouths connected. But instead she melded her body right to his and his arms reached out to hold her around the waist. As soon as she was reacquainted with his taste, her tongue latched onto his and began a sensuous duel that had her moaning.

In all her attempts at logical thinking over the past month, not until now could she admit how much she'd missed him. How much she'd missed this. How could a man engrain himself inside a woman's senses so deeply and thoroughly, and so quickly? And how could any woman resist this particular man doing so?

She heard the door click and knew he'd maneuvered her into her apartment and closed the door behind him. Noticing that, she almost pulled back, and she would have had he not at that moment deepened the kiss.

This had to be a dream. Is that why the room felt as if it was spinning? There was no way Aidan was in Laramie, at her apartment and kissing her. But if this was a dream she wasn't ready to wake up. She needed to get her fill of his taste before her fantasy faded. Before she realized in horror that she was actually kissing the short and bald mailman instead of Aidan. Had her fascination with him finally gotten the best of her?

The thought had her breaking off the kiss and opening her eyes. The man standing across from her with lips damp from their kiss was definitely Aidan.

She drew in a deep breath, trying to slow the beat of her heart and regain control of her senses.

As if he'd known just what she was thinking, he said, "It's really me, Jillian. And I'm here to help you study for your MCAT this week."

She blinked. *Help her study?* He had to be kidding.

Aidan wanted nothing more than to kiss the shocked look off Jillian's face. But he knew that before he could even think about kissing her again he had a lot of explaining to do since he'd gone back on their agreement.

"I talked to Dillon a few days ago and he mentioned you wouldn't be coming home for spring break and the reason why. So I figured I could help by giving you a good study boost."

She shook her head as if doing so would clear her mind. Looking back at him, she said, "There's no way you could have thought that. And what was that kiss about? I thought we had an understanding."

"We did. We still do. However, based on the way you responded to my kiss just now, I think we might need to modify a few things."

She lifted her chin. "There's nothing for us to modify."

That response irritated him to the core. "Do you think I want to be here, Jillian? I have a life in Boston, a life I was enjoying until recently. Ever since the kisses we shared on your birthday, I've done nothing but think about you, want you, miss you."

"That's not my fault," she snapped.

"It is when you're not being honest with yourself. Can you look me in the eyes and tell me that you haven't thought of me? That you haven't been wanting me? And be honest for once because if you deny it then you need to tell me why your kiss just now said otherwise."

He watched as she nervously licked her tongue across her lips and his gut clenched. "Tell me, Jillian," he said in a softer tone. "For once be honest with me and with yourself."

She drew in a long breath as they stared at each other. After several tense moments passed between them, she said, "Okay, I have been thinking of you, missing you, wanting you. And I hated myself for doing so. You're a weakness I can't afford to have right now. It's crazy. I know a lot of guys around campus. But why you? Why do I want the one guy I can't have?"

Her words softened his ire. She was just as confused

and frustrated as he was. "And why do you think you can't have me?"

She frowned. "You know why, Aidan. Pam and Dillon would be against it. In their eyes, we're family. And even if you were a guy she would approve of, she would try to convince me not to get involved with you and to stay focused on becoming a doctor."

"You don't know for certain that's how she would feel, Jillian."

"I do know. When Pam was in college pursuing her dream of becoming an actress, I asked her why she didn't date. She told me that a woman should never sacrifice her dream for any man."

"I'm not asking you to sacrifice your dream."

"No, but you want an involvement during a time when I should be more focused than ever on becoming a doctor."

"I want to help you, not hinder you," he stressed again.

"How do you think you can do that?"

At least she was willing to listen. "By using this week to introduce you to study techniques that will help you remember those things you need to remember."

She nervously licked her tongue across her lips again. "It won't work. I won't be able to think straight with you around."

"I'll make sure you do. I'm not asking to stay here, Jillian. I've already checked into a hotel a mile or so from here. I'll arrive every morning and we'll study until evening, taking short breaks in between. Then we'll grab something to eat and enjoy the evening. Afterward, I'll bring you back here and then leave. Before going to bed you should review what was covered that day, making sure you get eight hours of sleep."

She looked at him as if he was crazy. "I can't take time from studying to enjoy the evening. I'll need to study morning, noon and night."

"Not with me helping you. Besides, too much studying will make you burned out, and you don't want to do that. What good is studying if that happens?"

When she didn't say anything, he pushed harder. "Try my way for a couple of days and if it doesn't work, if you feel I'm more of a hindrance than a help, I'll leave Laramie and let you do things your way."

As she stared at him, not saying anything, he could feel blood throb through his veins. As usual she looked serious. Beautiful. Tempting. He wanted her. Being around her would be hard and leaving her every night after dinner would be harder. He would want to stay and make love to her all through the night. But that wasn't possible. No matter how hard it would be, he needed to keep his self-control.

"Okay," she finally said. "We'll try it for a couple of days. And if it doesn't work I intend for you to keep your word about leaving."

"I will." He had no intention of leaving because he intended for his plan to work. He had aced the MCAT the first time around, with flying colors. Once he'd gotten his act together as a teenager, he'd discovered he was an excellent test taker, something Adrian was not. Determined not to leave his twin behind, he'd often tutored Adrian, sharing his study tips and techniques with his brother. Aidan had also done the same with Bailey once she was in college. Unfortunately, he'd never gotten the chance to share his techniques with Bane since his cousin hadn't been interested in anything or anyone but Crystal.

"Now let's seal our agreement," he said.

When she extended her hand, he glanced at it before pulling her into his arms again.

He was taking advantage again, Jillian thought. But she only thought that for a second. That was all the time it took for her to begin returning his kiss with the same hunger he seemed to feel. This was crazy. It was insane. It was also what she needed. What she'd been wanting since leaving Denver and returning to Laramie.

Kissing was something they enjoyed doing with each other and the unhurried mating of their mouths definitely should be ruled illegal. But for now she could handle this—in the safety of her living room, in the arms of a man she thoroughly enjoyed kissing—as long as it went no further.

But what if it did? He'd already shown her that his definition of kissing included any part of her body. What if he decided he wanted more than her mouth this time? Her hormones were going haywire just thinking of the possibility.

He suddenly broke off the kiss and she fought back a groan of disappointment. She stared up at him. "Okay, where's the study guide?" he asked her.

She blinked. Her mind was slow in functioning after such a blazing kiss. It had jarred her senses. "Study guide?"

He smiled and caressed her cheek. "Yes, the MCAT study guide."

"On my kitchen table. I was studying when you showed up."

"Good. And you'll study some more. Lead the way."

* * *

Aidan leaned back in his chair and glanced over at Jillian. "Any questions?"

She shook her head. "No, but you make it seem simple."

He smiled. "Trust me, it's not. The key is to remember that you're the one in control of your brain and the knowledge that's stored inside of it. Don't let retrieving that information during test time psych you out."

She chuckled. "That's easy for you to say."

"And it will be easy for you, as well. I've been there, and when time allows I tutor premed students like yourself. You did well on the practice exam, which covers basically everything you need to know. Now you need to concentrate on those areas you're not so sure about."

"Which is a lot."

"All of them are things you know," he countered. He believed the only reason she lacked confidence in her abilities was because the idea of failing was freaking her out. "You don't have to pass on the first go-round. A lot of people don't. That's why it's suggested you plan to take it at least twice."

She lifted her chin. "I want to ace it on the first try."

"Then do it."

Aidan got up from his chair and went over to the coffeepot sitting on her kitchen counter. He needed something stronger than caffeine, but coffee would have to do. He'd been here for five hours already and they hadn't stopped for lunch. The key was to take frequent short breaks instead of one or two long ones.

She had taken the online practice exam on verbal reasoning and he thought she'd done well for her first time. He'd given her study tips for multiple-choice exams and gone over the questions she had missed. Personally, he thought she would do fine, although he thought taking the test in two months was pushing it. He would have suggested three months instead of two.

"Want some coffee?" he asked, pouring himself a cup.

"No, I'm okay."

Yes, she definitely was. He couldn't attest to her mental state with all that she'd crammed into that brain of hers today, but he could definitely attest to her physical one. She looked amazing, even with her hair tied back in a ponytail and a cute pair of reading glasses perched on her nose. He was used to seeing her without makeup and preferred her that way. She had natural beauty with her flawless creamy brown skin. And she looked cute in her jeans and top.

He glanced at his watch. "Jillian?"

She glanced up from the computer and looked over at him. "Yes?"

"It's time to call it a day."

She seemed baffled by his statement. "Call it a day? I haven't covered everything I wanted to do today."

"You covered a lot and you don't want to overload your brain."

She stared at him for a moment and then nodded and began shutting down her computer. "Maybe you're right. Thanks to you, I did cover a lot. Definitely a lot more than I would have if you hadn't been here. You're a great tutor."

"And you're a good student." He glanced at his watch again. "What eating places do you have around here?"

"Depends on what you have a taste for."

He had a taste for her, but knew he had to keep his promise and not push her into anything. "A juicy steak."

"Then you're in luck," she said, standing. "There's a great steak place a few blocks from here. Give me a few minutes to change."

"Okay." He watched her hurry off toward her bedroom.

When she closed the door behind her, he rubbed a hand down his face. Jillian was temptation even when she wasn't trying to be. When he'd asked about her roommate she'd told him that Ivy had gone home for spring break. That meant...

Nothing. Unless she made the first move or issued an invitation. Until then, he would spend his nights alone at the hotel.

Eight

Jillian glanced across the table at Aidan. It was day three and still hard to believe that he was in Laramie, that he had come to give her a kick-start in her studying. Day one had been frustrating. He'd pushed her beyond what she thought she was ready for. But going to dinner with him that night had smoothed her ruffled feathers.

Dinner had been fun. She'd discovered he enjoyed eating his steaks medium rare and he loved baked potatoes loaded with sour cream, bacon bits and cheddar cheese. He also loved unsweetened tea and when it came to anything with chocolate, he could overdose if he wasn't careful.

He was also a great conversationalist. He engaged her in discussions about everything—but he deemed the topic of medical school to be off-limits. They talked about the economy, recent elections, movies they had enjoyed, and about Adrian's plans to travel the world a few years after getting his PhD in engineering.

And Aidan got her talking. She told him about Ivy, who she thought was the roommate from heaven; about Jillian's decision two years ago to move out of the dorm; and about her first experience with a pushy car salesman. She told him about all the places she wanted to visit one day and that the one thing she wanted to do and hadn't done yet was go on a cruise.

It occurred to her later that it had been the first time she and Aidan had shared a meal together alone, and she had enjoyed it. It had made her even more aware of him as a man. She'd had the time to look beyond his handsome features and she'd discovered he was a thoughtful and kind person. He had been pleasant, treating everyone with respect, including the waitress and servers. And each time he smiled at her, her stomach clenched. Then he would take a sip of his drink, and she would actually envy his straw.

After dinner they returned to her apartment. He made her promise that she would only review what they'd covered that day and not stay up past nine, then he left. But not before taking her into his arms and giving her a kiss that rendered her weak and senseless—to the point where she was tempted to ask him to stay longer. But she fought back the temptation. Knowing she would see him again the next day had made falling asleep quick and easy. For the first time in a long time, she had slept through the night, though he'd dominated her dreams.

He arrived early the next morning with breakfast, which she appreciated. Then it was back to studying again. The second day had been more intense than the first. Knowing they couldn't cover every aspect of the study guide in one week, he had encouraged her to hit the areas she felt were her weakest. He gave her hints on how to handle multiple-choice questions and introduced her to key words to use when completing her essays.

For dinner they had gone to the Wild Duck. She had been eager to introduce him to her favorite place. A dinner of hamburgers, French fries and milk shakes had been wonderful. Afterward they went to Harold's Game Hall to shoot pool, something she had learned to do in high school.

When he'd brought her home, like the night before, he took her in his arms and kissed her before he left, giving her the same instructions about reviewing what they'd covered that morning and getting eight hours of sleep. Again, she'd slept like a baby with him dominating her dreams.

She enjoyed having him as a study coach. Most of the time she stayed focused. But there were a few times when she felt heat simmering between them, something both of them tried to ignore. They managed it most of the time but today was harder than the two days before.

Aidan was tense. She could tell. He had arrived that morning, like yesterday, with breakfast in hand. Since he believed she should study on a full stomach and not try eating while studying, they had taken their meal outside to her patio. It had been pleasant, but more than once she'd caught him staring at her with a look in his eyes that she felt in the pit of her stomach.

He wasn't as talkative today as he'd been the past two days, and, taking a cue from his mood, she hadn't said much, either. On those occasions when their hands had accidentally touched while he'd been handing her papers or turning a page, she wasn't sure who sizzled more, her or him.

That's why she'd made up her mind about how today would end. She wanted him and he wanted her and there was no reason for them to suffer with their desires any longer. She'd fallen in love with him. After this time together, she could admit that now. That little crush she'd had on him for years had become something more. Something deeper and more profound.

The thought of Pam and Dillon finding out was still an issue that plagued her. However, since Aidan didn't feel the same way about her that she felt about him, she was certain she would be able to convince him to keep whatever they did a secret. He was doing that now anyway. He'd told her that neither Pam nor Dillon knew where he was spending this week. That meant Jillian and Aidan were already keeping secrets from their family, and she would continue to do so if it meant spending more time with him.

That night they went to a restaurant she had never visited because of its pricey menu. The signature dishes had been delicious and the service excellent. But the restaurant's setting spoke of not only elegance but also romance. Rustic wood ceilings with high beams, a huge brick fireplace and a natural stone floor. Beautiful candles adorned the tables and even in the dim light, each time she glanced over at Aidan he was looking back at her.

Getting through dinner hadn't been easy. They conversed but not as much as they had the previous two nights. Was she imagining things or did his voice sound deeper, huskier than usual? His smiles weren't full ones but half smiles, and just as sexy.

Like he'd done the previous two nights, he walked through her apartment, checking to make sure everything was okay. Then he gave her orders to only review what she'd studied that morning and get into bed before nine because at least eight hours of sleep were essential.

And then, as had become his habit, he pulled her into his arms to kiss her goodbye. This is what she had anticipated all day. She was ready for Aidan's kiss. Standing on tiptoe she tilted her open mouth toward him, her tongue ready. He closed his full mouth over hers and their tongues tangled, almost bringing her to her knees.

The kiss lasted for a long, delectable moment. It was different than any they'd shared before and she'd known it the moment their mouths fused. It was hot, heavy and hungry. He wasn't letting up or backing down—and neither was she.

Jillian felt herself being lifted off her feet and she immediately wrapped her legs around his waist while he continued to ravish her mouth in a way that overwhelmed her and overloaded her senses. His hunger was sexual and greedy. She could tell he was fighting hard to hold it together, to stay in control, to keep his sanity in check. But she wasn't. In fact, she was deliberately trying to tempt him every way that she could.

She felt the wall at her back and knew he'd maneuvered them over to it. He broke off the kiss and stared at her, impaling her with the flaming fire in his eyes. "Tell me to stop, Jillian," he said. "Because if you don't do it now, I won't be able to stop later. I want to tongue you all over. Lick every inch of your body. Taste you. Make love to you. Hard. Long. Deep. So tell me to stop now."

Her pulse jumped. Every single cell in her body sizzled with his words. Hot, sparks of passion glowed in his gaze and when a powerful burst of primal need slammed through her she didn't want to escape.

"Tell me to stop."

His plea made the already hot sexual tension between them blaze, and she knew of only one way to put out the fire.

"Stop, Aidan!"

His body went still. The only thing that moved was the pulse throbbing in his throat. He held her gaze and she was convinced she could hear blood rushing through both of their veins.

When she felt him about to untangle her legs from around his waist and lower her feet to the floor, she said, "Stop talking and do all those things you claim you're going to do."

She saw the impact of her words reflected in his eyes. While he seemed incapable of speaking, she released her arms from around his neck and tugged at his shirt, working her hands beneath to touch his bare chest. She heard the groan from deep in his throat.

"If you don't take me, Aidan Westmoreland, then I'll be forced to take you."

That was the last thing Aidan had expected her to say. But hearing her say it intensified the throbbing need within him. His crotch pounded fiercely and he knew of only one way to remedy that. But first...

He lowered her to her feet as a smile tugged at his lips. Only for a moment, he gazed down at her shirt, noticing the curve of her breasts beneath the cotton. In an instant, he tugged the shirt over her head and tossed it aside.

He drew in a deep breath when his eyes settled on her chest, specifically her skin-tone colored bra. Eager beyond belief, he touched her breasts through the lace material. When his fingers released the front clasp, causing the twin globes to spring free, the breath was snatched from his lungs.

Mercy. He eased the bra straps from her shoulders to remove it completely from her body and his mouth watered. Her breasts were one area that he hadn't tasted yet, and he planned on remedying that soon.

Deciding he wanted to see more naked flesh, he lowered to his knees and slid his fingers beneath the elastic waistband of her skirt to ease it down her legs. She stepped out of it and he tossed it aside to join her shirt and bra. His gaze raked the full length of her body, now only covered by a pair of light blue bikini panties. His hands actually trembled when he ran them down her legs. He felt as if he were unveiling a precious treasure.

She stepped out of them as she'd done her skirt and she stood in front of him totally naked. He leaned back on his haunches while his gaze raked her up and down, coming back to her center. He was tempted to start right there, but he knew if he did that, he wouldn't get to taste her breasts this time, either, and he refused to miss the chance again.

Standing back on his feet, Aidan leaned and lowered his head. He captured a nipple between his lips, loving how the tip hardened in his mouth as his tongue traced circles around the rigid bud. She purred his name as she cradled the back of his head to hold his mouth right there.

He continued to taste her breasts, leaving one and moving to the other, enjoying every single lick and suck. Her moans fueled his desire to possess her. To make love to her. And what he loved more than anything else was the sound of her moaning his name.

Aidan eased his lips from her breasts and moved his mouth slowly downward, tasting her skin. As he crouched, his mouth traced a greedy path over her stomach, loving the way her muscles tightened beneath his lips.

A slow throbbing ache took hold of his erection as he eased down to his knees. This was what he'd gone to bed craving ever since he'd first tasted her between her thighs. He'd fallen asleep several nights licking his lips at the memory. Her feminine scent was unique, so irresistibly Jillian, that his tongue thickened in anticipation.

Knowing she watched him, he ran his hands up and down the insides of her legs, massaged her thighs and caressed the area between them. His name was a whisper on her lips when he slid a finger inside of her. He loved the feel of her juices wetting him. He stroked her.

Hungry for her taste, he withdrew his finger and licked it. He smiled before using his hands to spread her feminine core to ready her for an open-mouth kiss.

Jillian released a deep, toe-curling moan the moment Aidan latched his hot tongue onto her. She grabbed his head to push him away, but he held tight to her legs while his tongue went deep, thrusting hard. Then she pressed herself toward his mouth.

She closed her eyes and chanted his name as spasms ripped through her, making her thighs tremble. He refused to let go, refused to lift his mouth, as sensations overtook her. Her body throbbed in unexpected places as an orgasm shook her.

When the last spasm speared through her, she felt herself being lifted into strong arms. When she opened her eyes, Aidan was entering her bedroom. He placed her on the bed, leaned down and kissed her, sending rekindled desire spiking through her.

When he ended the kiss and eased off the bed, she watched as he quickly removed his clothes. She could only lie there and admire his nakedness. He was a fine specimen of a man, both in and out of clothes. Just as he'd appeared in her dreams. Thick thighs, muscular legs and a huge erection nested in a patch of thick, curly black hair.

How will I handle that? she asked herself when he pulled a condom packet from his wallet and quickly sheathed himself. He took his time and she figured it was because he knew she was watching his every move with keen interest.

"You have done this before right?" he asked her.

"What? Put on a condom? No. One wouldn't fit me."

He grinned over at her. "Funny. You know what I'm asking."

Yes, she knew what he was asking. "Um, sort of."

He lifted a brow. "Sort of?"

She shrugged slightly. "I'm not a virgin, if that's what you're asking," she said softly. "Technically not. But…"

"But what?"

"I was in high school and neither of us knew what we were doing. That was my one and only time."

He just stood there totally naked staring at her. She wondered why he wasn't saying anything. What was he thinking? As if he'd read her mind, he slowly moved toward her, placed his knee on the bed and leaned toward her. "What you missed out on before, you will definitely get tonight. And Jillian?"

She swallowed. He'd spoken with absolute certainty and all she could do was stare back at him. "Yes?"

"This will not be your only time with me."

Her body reacted to his words and liquid heat traveled through her body. He hadn't spoken any words of love but he'd let her know this wasn't a one-time deal with them.

She didn't have time to dwell on what he'd said. He pulled her into his arms and kissed her. She closed her eyes and let herself be liquefied by the kiss. Like all the other times he'd used his expertise to make everything around her fade into oblivion, the kiss was the only thing her mind and body could comprehend. His hands were all over her, touching her everywhere. She released a deep moan when she felt his knees spreading her legs.

"Open your eyes and look at me Jillian."

She slowly opened her eyes to look up at the man whose body was poised above hers. He lifted her hips and his enlarged sex slid between her wet feminine folds. He thrust forward and her body stretched to accommodate his size. Instinctively, she wrapped her legs around him and when he began to move, she did so, as well.

She continued to hold his gaze while he thrust in and out of her. Over and over he would take her to the edge just to snatch her back. Her inner muscles clamped down on him, squeezing and tightening around him.

As she felt new spasms rip through her, he threw his head back and let out a roar that shook the room. She was glad most of her neighbors had gone away for spring break; otherwise they would know what she was doing tonight.

But right now, all she cared about was the man she loved, and how he was making her feel things she'd never felt before.

He kissed her again. Their tongues dueled in another erotic kiss and she couldn't help but remember the words he'd spoken earlier.

This will not be your only time with me.

She knew men said words they didn't mean to women

they were about to sleep with, and she had no reason to believe it was any different with Aidan.

Besides, considering that she needed to stay focused on her studies, it was a good thing he wasn't serious.

Aidan watched the naked woman sleeping in his arms and let out a frustrated sigh. This was not supposed to happen.

He wasn't talking about making love because there was no way such a thing could have been avoided. The sexual tension between them had been on overload since the day he'd arrived at her apartment and neither of them could have lasted another day.

What was *not* supposed to happen was feeling all these unexpected emotions. They had wrapped around his mind and wouldn't let go. And what bothered him more than anything else was that he knew he was not confusing his emotions with what had definitely been off-the-charts sex. If he hadn't known before that there was a difference in what he felt for Jillian, he definitely knew it now.

He had fallen in love with her.

When? How? Why? He wasn't sure. All he knew, without a doubt, was that it had happened. The promise of great sex hadn't made him take a week's vacation and travel more than fifteen hundred miles across five states to spend time with her. Sex hadn't made him become her personal test coach, suffering the pains of being close to her while maintaining boundaries and limits. And sex definitely had nothing to do with the way he felt right now and how it was nearly impossible for him to think straight.

When she purred softly in her sleep and then wiggled

her backside snugly against his groin he closed his eyes and groaned. It had been great sex but it had been more than that. She had reached a part of him no woman had reached before.

He'd realized it before they'd made love. He'd known it the minute she told him she'd only made love once before. As far as he was concerned that one time didn't count because the guy had definitely done a piss-poor job. The only orgasm she'd ever experienced had been with Aidan.

But in the days he'd spent studying with her he'd gotten to know a lot about her. She was a fighter, determined to reach whatever goals she established for herself. And she was thoughtful enough to care that Pam not bear the burden of the cost of sending Jillian to medical school. She was even willing to sell her family home.

And he liked being with her, which posed a problem since they lived more than a thousand miles apart. He'd heard long-distance affairs could sometimes be brutal. But he and Jillian could make it work if they wanted to do so. He knew how he felt about her but he had no idea how she felt about him. As far as he knew, she wasn't operating on emotion but out of a sense of curiosity. She'd said as much.

However, the biggest problem of all, one he knew would pose the most challenge to the possibility of anything ever developing between them was her insistence on Pam and Dillon not knowing about them.

Aidan didn't feel the same way and now that he loved her, he really didn't want to keep it a secret. He knew Dillon well enough to know that if Aidan were to go to his cousin and come clean, tell Dillon Aidan had fallen in love with Jillian, Dillon would be okay with it. Although

Aidan couldn't say with certainty how Pam would feel, he'd always considered her a fair person. He believed she would eventually give her blessing…but only if she thought Jillian was truly in love with him and that he would make Jillian happy.

There were so many unknowns. The one thing he did know was that he and Jillian had to talk. He'd given her fair warning that what they'd shared would not be one and done. There was no way he would allow her to believe that her involvement with him meant nothing, that she was just another woman to him. She was more than that and he wanted her to know it.

She stirred, shifted in bed and then slowly opened her eyes to stare at him. She blinked a few times as if bringing him into focus—or as if she was trying to figure out if he was really here in her bed.

Aidan let her know she wasn't seeing things. "Good morning." He gently caressed her cheek before glancing over at the digital clock on her nightstand. "You woke up early. It's barely six o'clock."

"A habit I can't break," she said, still staring at him. "You didn't leave."

"Was I supposed to?"

She shrugged bare shoulders. "I thought that's the way it worked."

She had a lot to learn about him. He wouldn't claim he'd never left a woman's bed in the middle of the night, but Jillian was different.

"Not for us, Jillian." He paused. "We need to talk."

She broke eye contact as she pulled up in bed, holding the covers in place to shield her nakedness. Aidan thought the gesture amusing considering all they'd done last night. "I know what you're going to say, Aidan. Although I've never heard it before, Ivy has and she told me how this plays out."

She'd made him curious. "And how does it play out?"

"The guy lets the woman know it was just a one-night stand. Nothing personal and definitely nothing serious."

He hadn't used that particular line before, but he'd used similar ones. He decided not to tell her that. "You weren't a one-night stand, Jillian."

She nodded. "I do recall you mentioning that last night wouldn't be your only time with me."

He tightened his arms around her. "And why do you think I said that?"

"Because you're a man and most men enjoy sex."

He smiled. "A lot of women enjoy it, as well. Didn't you?"

"Yes. There's no need to lie about it. I definitely enjoyed it."

A grin tugged at Aidan's lips. His ego appreciated her honesty. "I enjoyed it, as well." He kissed her, needing the taste of her.

It was a brief kiss and when he lifted his lips from hers, she seemed stunned by what he'd done. He found that strange considering the number of times they had kissed before.

"So, if you don't want to say last night was a one-night stand, what is it you want to talk about?" she asked.

He decided to be just as honest as she had been, and got straight to the point. "I want to talk about me. And you. Together."

She raised a brow. "Together?"

"Yes. I've fallen in love with you."

Nine

Jillian was out of the bed in a flash, taking half the blankets with her. She speared Aidan with an angry look. "Are you crazy? You can't be in love with me. It won't work, especially when I'm in love with you, too."

Too late she'd realized what she'd said. From the look on Aidan's face, he had heard her admission. "If I love you and you love me, Jillian, then what's the problem?"

She lifted her chin. "The problem is that we can't be together the way you would want us to be. I was okay with it when it was one-sided and I just loved you and didn't think you could possibly return the feelings, but now—"

"Hold up," Aidan said, and her eyes widened when he got off the bed to stand in front of her without a stitch of clothes on. "Let me get this straight. You think it's okay for me to sleep with you and not be in love with you?"

She tossed her hair back from her face. "Why not? I'm sure it's done all the time. Men sleep with women they don't love and vice versa. Are you saying you love every woman you sleep with?"

"No."

"Okay then."

"It's not okay because you're not any woman. You're the one that I *have* fallen in love with."

Why was he making things difficult? Downright complicated? She had to make him understand. "I could deal with this a lot better if you didn't love me, mainly because I would have known it wasn't serious on your end."

"And that would not have bothered you?"

"Not in the least. I need to stay focused on my studies and I can't stay focused if I know you feel the same way about me that I feel about you. That only complicates things."

He stared at her as if he thought she was crazy. In a way she couldn't very much blame him. Most women would prefer falling in love with a man who loved them, and if things were different she would want that, too. But the time wasn't right. Men in love made demands. They expected a woman's time. Her attention. All her energy. And being in love required that a woman give her man what he wanted. Well, she didn't have the time to do that. She was in medical school. She wanted to be a doctor.

And worse than anything, an Aidan who thought he loved her would cause problems. He wouldn't want to keep their relationship a secret. He was not a man to be kept in the closet or denied his right to be seen with her. He would want everyone to know they were together and that was something she couldn't accept.

"I still can't understand why you think me loving you complicates things," Aidan said, interrupting her thoughts.

"Because you wouldn't want to keep our affair a secret. You'll want to tell everyone. Take me out anyplace you want. You wouldn't like the thought of us sneaking around."

"No, I wouldn't." He gently pulled her into his arms. She would have pushed him away if he hadn't at that moment tugged the bedcovers from her hands leaving her as naked as he was. The moment their bodies touched, arousal hit her in the core. She was suddenly reminded of what they'd done last night and how they'd done it. From the way his eyes darkened, she knew he was reliving those same sizzling memories.

"Jillian."

"Aidan."

He drew her closer and closed his mouth over hers. She was lost. For a long while, all she could do was stand there feeling his body plastered to hers, feeling his erection pressed against her, feeling the tips of her nipples poking into his chest while he kissed her. Frissons of fire raced up her spine.

And when she felt herself being maneuvered toward the bed, she was too caught up in desire to do anything about it. The same urgency to mate that had taken hold of him had fused itself to her. As soon as her back touched the mattress she slid from beneath him and pushed him back. She had flipped them and was now on top of him. He stared up at her with surprise in his eyes.

She intended to play out one of her fantasies, one of the ways they'd made love in her dreams—with her on top. But first she needed him to know something. "I take the Pill…to regulate my periods. And I'm safe," she whispered.

"So am I."

She maneuvered her middle over his engorged shaft, which stood straight up. Every hormone inside her body sizzled as she eased down onto him, taking him inside inch by inch. He was big, but like last night her body stretched to accommodate his size.

"Look at me, Jillian." Obeying his command, she held his gaze.

"I love you, whether you want me to or not and it's too late for you to do anything about it."

She drew in a deep breath and continued to ease him inside of her, not wanting to dwell on the problems love could cause. They would talk again later. But for now, this is what she wanted. This is what she needed. And when she had taken him to the hilt, she moved, riding him the way she'd been taught to ride years ago. From the look reflected in the depths of his eyes, she was giving him a ride he would remember for a long time.

She liked the view from up here. Staring down at him, seeing his expression change each time she shoved downward, taking him deeper. His nostrils flared. His breathing was choppy. Was that a little sweat breaking through on his brow?

Riding him felt good. Exhilarating. He definitely had the perfect body to be ridden. Hard, masculine and solid. She had her knees locked on each side of his strong thighs. Her inner muscles clenched, gripping him in a hold that had him groaning deep in his throat.

She loved the sound. Loved being in control. Loved him. The last thought sent her senses spiraling, and when he shouted her named and bucked his entire body upward, she felt his massive explosion. He drenched her insides with thick semen. And she used her muscles to squeeze out more.

Perspiration soaked her head, her face, their bodies… but she kept on riding. When another explosion hit him, she nearly jerked them both off the bed when she screamed in pleasure.

He held her tight and she held him and she wished she never had to let him go.

Aidan pushed a damp curl out of Jillian's eyes. She was sprawled on top of him, breathing deeply. He figured she had earned the right to be exhausted. He'd never experienced anything so invigorating or stimulating in his entire life.

"Don't ask me not to love you, Jillian," he finally found the strength to say softly, and the words came straight from his heart. For the first time in his life, he'd told a woman he loved her and the woman wished that he didn't.

When he felt her tears fall on his arm, he shifted their bodies so he could look at her. "Is me loving you that bad?"

She shook her head. "No. I know it should be what I want but the timing… There is so much I still have to do."

"And you think I'd stop you from doing them?"

"No, but I'd stop myself. I'd lose focus. You would want to be with me and I would want to be with you. In the open. I know you don't understand why I can't do that, but I can't."

She was right, he didn't understand. He believed she was all wrong about how Dillon and Pam, or the entire Westmoreland family, would handle them hooking up. He doubted it would be a big deal. But it didn't matter what he thought. She thought otherwise and that's what mattered.

"What if I agree to do what we're doing now? I mean, keeping things between us a secret."

She lifted her head. "You would agree to that, Aidan? I'm not talking about a few weeks or a few months. I'm talking about until I finish medical school. Could you really wait that long?"

That was a good question. Could he? Could he be around Jillian at family gatherings and pretend nothing was going on between them? And what about the physical distance between them? She wasn't even sure what medical school she would attend. Her two top choices were Florida and New Orleans, both hundreds of miles away from Boston, Maine or North Carolina.

And what about his family and friends? Like Adrian, Aidan had quite a reputation around Harvard. What would his friends think when he suddenly stopped pursuing women? They would think he'd lost his ever-loving mind. But he didn't care what anyone thought.

It didn't matter. Wherever Jillian was, he would get to her, spend time with her and give her the support she needed to be the doctor she wanted to be.

What Jillian needed now more than anything was for him not to place any pressure on her. Her focus should be on completing the MCAT and not on anything else. Somehow he would handle the distance, he would handle his family and friends and their perceptions.

He held her gaze. "Yes, I can wait. No matter how long it takes, Jillian. Because you're worth waiting for."

Then he tugged her mouth down to his for another one of their ultrapassionate, mind-blowing kisses.

Ten

"This is Captain Stewart Marcellus," a deep voice boomed through the intercom in Jillian's cabin. "My crew and I would like to welcome you aboard the Princess Grandeur. For the next fourteen days we'll cruise the Grand Mediterranean for your enjoyment. In an hour we'll depart Barcelona for full days in Monte Carlo and Florence and two days in Rome. From there we'll sail to Greece and Turkey. I invite you to join me tonight at the welcome party, which kicks off two weeks of fun."

Jillian glanced around her cabin. *A suite.* This was something she definitely hadn't paid for. She and Paige had planned to share a standard stateroom, definitely nothing as luxurious and spacious as what she'd been given. When she'd contacted the customer service desk to tell them about the mistake, she was told no mistake had been made and the suite was hers to enjoy.

No sooner had she ended the call than she'd received a delivery—a bouquet of beautiful mixed flowers and a bottle of chilled wine with a card that read, "Congratulations on finishing medical school. We are proud of you. Enjoy the cruise. You deserve it. Your family, The Westmorelands."

Jillian eased down to sit on the side of the bed. *Her family.* She wondered what the Westmorelands would think if they knew the truth about her and Aidan. About the affair the two of them had carried on right under their noses for three years.

As she stood to shower and get dressed for tonight's festivities, she couldn't help remembering what that affair had been like after they'd confessed their love for each other. Aidan had understood and agreed that it was to be their secret. No one else was supposed to know— unless the two of them thought it was absolutely necessary.

The first year had been wonderful, in spite of how hard it had been to engage in a long-distance love affair. Even with Aidan's busy schedule juggling dual residencies, he'd managed to fly to Laramie whenever he had a free weekend. And because their time together was scarce, he'd make it special. They would go out to dinner, see a movie, or if it was a weekend she needed to study, they would do that, too. There was no way she would have passed the MCAT the first time around without his help. She had applied to various medical schools and when she was notified of her acceptance into the one she wanted in New Orleans, Aidan had been the first person with whom she'd shared her good news. They had celebrated the next time he'd come to Laramie.

It was during that first year that they agreed to bring Ivy in on their secret. Otherwise, her roommate would have been worried when Jillian went missing because she was staying with Aidan at the hotel.

Jillian had fallen more and more in love with Aidan

during that time. Although she'd had a lot to keep her busy, she missed him when they were apart. But he'd made up for it when he came to town. And even though they'd spent a lot of time in bed making love, their relationship wasn't just about sex. However, she would have to say that the sex was off the chain, and the sexual tension between them was still so thick you could cut it with a knife. Ivy could attest to that and had teased Jillian about it all the time.

It was also during that first year that their control had been tested whenever they went home for holidays, weddings or baby christenings. She would be the first to admit she had felt jealous more than a few times when Aidan's single male cousins, who assumed he was still a player on the prowl, would try setting him up with other women.

Everything had gone well between them as they moved into their second year together. Aidan had helped her relocate to New Orleans after she bid a teary goodbye to Ivy. Jillian leased a one-bedroom efficiency apartment not far from the hospital where she would be working. It was perfect for her needs, but lonely.

It was during the third year that it became harder for Aidan to get away. The hospitals demanded more of his time. And her telephone conversations with him had been reduced from nightly to three times a week. She could tell he was frustrated with the situation. More than once he'd commented that he wished she would have applied to a medical school closer to Maine or North Carolina.

Jillian tried to ignore his attitude but found that difficult to do. Although Aidan didn't say so, deep down she knew the secrecy surrounding their affair was getting to him. It had begun to get to her, as well. And when it seemed Aidan was becoming distant, she knew she had to do something.

When Ivy came to visit Jillian in New Orleans one weekend, she talked to her best friend about the situation. Even now Jillian could remember that time as if it was yesterday...

"So, how is Aidan?" Ivy asked, after placing her order with their waitress.

Jillian had to fight back tears. "Not sure. We haven't talked in a few days and the last time we did, we had an argument."

Ivy raised a brow. "Another one?"

"Yes." She'd told Ivy about their last argument. He'd wanted her to fly to Maine for the weekend for his birthday. She had been excited about doing so until she'd checked her calendar and discovered that was the same weekend of her clinicals. Something she could not miss. Instead of understanding, he'd gotten upset with her and because of his lack of understanding, she'd gotten upset with him. Their most recent argument had started because he told her his twin now knew about them. He'd gotten angry when she'd accused him of breaking his promise and telling Adrian. He'd explained that he didn't have to tell his brother anything. He and his twin could detect each other's moods and feelings sometimes.

"I'm tired of arguing with him, Ivy, and a part of me knows the reason our relationship is getting so strained."

Ivy nodded. "Long-distance romances are hard to maintain, Jillian, and I'm sure the secrecy surrounding your affair isn't helping."

"Yes, I know, which is why I've made a few decisions."

Ivy lifted a brow. "About what?"

Jillian drew in a deep breath. "I've decided to tell Pam about us. The secrecy has gone on long enough. I believe my sister will accept the fact that I'm now an adult and old enough to decide what I want to do in my life and the person I want in it."

"Good for you."

"Thanks. I know she's been concerned about Aidan's womanizing reputation, but once she realizes that I love him and he loves me, I believe she will give us her blessing."

Jillian took a sip of her drink and continued, "But before I tell Pam, I'm flying to Maine to see Aidan. Next weekend is his birthday and I've decided to be there to help him celebrate."

"What about your clinicals?"

Jillian smiled. "I went to my professor and told her I desperately needed that weekend off. She agreed to work with me and arrange for me to do a makeup the following weekend."

"That was nice of her."

"Yes, it was. She said I was a good student, the first to volunteer for projects and my overall attendance is great. So now I'm set to go."

Ivy grinned. "Did you tell Aidan?"

"No. I'm going to surprise him. He mentioned that since I wouldn't be there to celebrate with him that he would sign up to work that day and then hang around his place, watch TV and go to bed early."

"On his birthday? That's a bummer."

"Yes, and that's why I plan to fly there to help him celebrate."

"You're doing the right thing by being there. I think it's wonderful that you're finally letting your sister know about you and Aidan. When she sees how much he adores you she will be happy for the two of you."

A huge smile touched Jillian's lips. "I believe so, too."

Jillian stepped out on the balcony to look at the ocean as she recalled what happened after that. She had been excited when she'd boarded the plane for Portland, Maine. She couldn't wait to tell Aidan of her decision to end the secrecy surrounding their affair and to celebrate his birthday with him.

Due to stormy weather in Atlanta, her connecting flight had been delayed five solid hours and she didn't arrive in Portland until six that evening. It had been another hour before she'd arrived at his apartment complex, anxious to use the door key he'd given her a year ago for the first time.

The moment she'd stepped off the elevator onto his floor she knew a party was going on in one of the apartments. Loud music blasted and boisterous voices made her ears ache. She hadn't known all the noise was coming from Aidan's apartment until she'd reached the door, which she didn't have to unlock since it was slightly ajar.

Jillian walked in and looked around. The place was crowded and there were more women in attendance than men. The women were wearing outfits that probably wouldn't be allowed out on the streets.

Jillian wondered what had happened to Aidan's decision to come home from work, watch TV and go to bed. It seemed he'd decided to throw a party instead and it was in full swing. In the center of the room Aidan sat in a recliner while some scantily dressed woman gave him a lap dance. And from the look on his face, he was enjoying every single minute of it. Some of the guys on the sidelines, who she figured must be Aidan's friends, were egging on both him and the woman, which prompted the woman to make the dance even more erotic.

When the woman began stripping off her clothes, starting with the barely-there strap of material covering her breasts, Jillian was shocked. She knew she'd seen enough when the woman's breasts all but smothered Aidan's face while she wiggled out of her panties.

Not able to watch any longer, a shaken Jillian had left, grateful Aidan hadn't even noticed her presence. What hurt more than anything was that he'd appeared to be enjoying every single minute of the dance. Aidan Westmoreland had seemed in his element. She couldn't help wondering if they had stopped with the dance or if he and the woman had ended up doing other things later.

When he'd called her a few days later he hadn't mentioned anything about the party at his apartment and she hadn't said anything about being there to witness what had gone on. And when she asked how he'd spent his birthday, he angered her even more when he gave her a smart aleck answer, asking, "Why do you care when you didn't care enough to spend it with me?"

He was wrong. She had cared enough. But he hadn't cared enough to tell her the truth. It was then that she'd made the decision to end things between them, since it was apparent that he missed his life as a womanizer. When he called later in the week and made another excuse for not flying to New Orleans to see her as he'd planned, she decided that would be a good time to break things off with him. She would give him his freedom, let him go back to the life he missed.

Deciding the less drama the better, she told him the secrecy of their affair was weighing her down, making her lose focus and she couldn't handle it any longer. She didn't tell him the true reason she'd wanted to end things.

Her declaration led to a huge argument between them. When he told her he was flying to New Orleans to talk to her, she told him she didn't want to see him. Then she ended the conversation.

He had called several times to talk to her but she'd refused to answer and eventually blocked his number. She knew that was the reason for the angry looks he'd given her when she'd attended the last couple of Westmoreland weddings. The last time she'd seen him was a few months ago at Stern's ceremony.

There had been no reason to tell Pam about the affair that had been a secret for so long, so she hadn't. The last thing Jillian needed was for her sister to remind her that just like a tiger couldn't change its stripes neither could a womanizer change his ways.

It had been a year since their breakup. At times she felt she had moved on, but other times she felt she had not. It was so disappointing and painful to think about the future they could have been planning together now that she'd finished medical school, if only things had worked out the way she'd hoped they would.

Jillian wiped the tears from her eyes, refusing to shed any more for Aidan. She was on this cruise to have fun and enjoy herself, and she intended to do just that.

"Yes, Adrian?"

"I'm glad I was able to reach you before ship left port.

I just want to wish you the best. I hope everything works out the way you want with Jill."

Aidan hoped things worked out the way he wanted, as well. "Thanks."

Like Paige, Adrian and Aidan's cousin Stern had figured out something was going on between him and Jillian a couple of years ago. "I will do whatever I have to do to get her back. When this ship returns to port, my goal is to have convinced Jillian to give me another chance."

"Well, Trinity and I are cheering for you."

"Thanks, bro." Trinity was Adrian's fiancée and the two would be getting married in a couple of months.

After ending his phone call with Adrian, Aidan crossed the suite to step out on the balcony. Barcelona was beautiful. He had arrived three days ago and taken a tour of what was considered one of the busiest ports in the Mediterranean. He had eaten at the finest restaurants, some in magnificent buildings etched deep with history. He had walked through the crowded streets wishing Jillian had been by his side. Hopefully when they returned to this port in fourteen days she would be.

He could just imagine what Jillian had assumed when she'd seen that woman giving him a lap dance last year. He had worked that day, as he'd told her he would, but he hadn't known about the surprise birthday party a few of his fraternity brothers had thrown for him.

And he definitely hadn't known about the lap dancer or the other strippers they'd invited until the women arrived. He couldn't get mad at his frat brothers for wanting to make his birthday kind of wild. All they knew was that for the past few years, the man who'd once been one of the biggest womanizers in Boston had taken a sabbatical from women. They'd had no idea that the reason for his seemingly boring lifestyle was because he was involved in a secret affair with Jillian.

So, thinking he'd been working too hard for too long and hadn't gotten in any play time, they thought they were doing him a favor. He would admit that after a few drinks he'd loosened up. But at no time had he forgotten he was in love with Jillian. The lap dance had been just for fun, and after the party all the women had left.

Yes, he'd made a mistake by not mentioning the party to Jillian. And he would be the first to admit his attitude had been less than desirable for the last year of their relationship. But he knew why. He'd had the best of intentions when he thought he could keep their secret without any problems, but as time went on, he'd become impatient. While she hadn't wanted anyone to know about them, he had wanted to shout the truth from the highest mountain.

It hadn't helped matters when some of his siblings and cousins began falling in love and getting married. It seemed as if an epidemic had hit Westmoreland Country when five of his relatives got married in a two-year period. And some had been relatives he'd thought would never marry. It had been hard being around his happily married kinfolk without wanting to have some of that happiness for himself. He would admit he'd spent too many months angry with himself, with Jillian, with the world. But at no time did he doubt his love for her.

Nothing had changed his feelings. He was still in love with her, which was why he was here. To right a wrong and convince her that she was the only woman he wanted.

He knew he had his work cut out for him. But he

intended to stay the course and not fail in his task. She wouldn't appreciate seeing him and she probably wouldn't like it when she found out about Paige's involvement. Or Ivy's for that matter. If Ivy hadn't told Paige the truth, he would still be angry, thinking the reason Jillian had broken up with him was because they were at odds regarding the secret of their affair.

He went back inside when he heard the cabin phone ring. He picked it up. "Yes?"

"I hope you find your quarters satisfactory."

Aidan smiled. That was an understatement. "It's more than satisfactory, Dominic."

This ship was just one of many in a fleet owned by Dominic Saxon. Dominic was married to the former Taylor Steele, whose sister Cheyenne was married to Aidan's cousin, Quade Westmoreland. Once Aidan discovered Jillian had booked her cruise on one of Dominic's ships, his friend had been all too eager to assist Aidan in getting back the woman he loved. Years ago Dominic had found himself in a similar situation.

"Taylor sends her love and we're all rooting for you. I know how misunderstandings can threaten even the most solid relationships, and I think you're doing the right thing by going after her," Dominic said. "I'm going to give you the same advice a very smart woman—my mother—gave me when I was going through my troubles with Taylor. *Let love guide you to do the right thing.* I hope the two of you enjoy the cruise."

"Thanks for the advice, and as for enjoying the cruise, I intend to make sure that we do."

After ending his call with Dominic, Aidan glanced around the cabin. Thanks to Dominic, Aidan had been given the owner's suite. It was spacious with a double balcony. There were also separate sleeping quarters with a king-size bed and a seventy-inch flat-screen television and a second wall-to-wall balcony. The sitting area contained a sofa that could convert into a double bed, another wall television and a dining area that overlooked yet another balcony. Other amenities he appreciated were the refrigerator, wet bar and huge walk-in closet. The bathroom was bigger than the one he had in his apartment, with both a Jacuzzi tub and a walk-in shower. He could just imagine him and Jillian using that shower together.

He walked back out on the balcony to see that people had gathered on the docks to watch the ship sail, waving flags that represented all the countries they would visit on the cruise. He expected Jillian to attend the welcome party tonight and so would he. Aidan couldn't wait to see Jillian's face when she discovered he was on board with her and would be for the next fourteen days.

He headed for the bathroom to shower.

Tonight couldn't get here fast enough.

"Welcome, senorita, may we assist with your mask?"

Jillian lifted a brow. "Mask?"

The tall crewman dressed in a crisp white uniform smiled down at her. "*Si.* Tonight's theme is a Spanish masquerade ball," he said, offering a red feathered mask to her.

She took it and slid it across her face. It was a perfect fit. "Thanks."

"Your name?" he asked.

"Jillian Novak."

"Senorita Novak, dinner will be served in a half hour

in the Madrid Room; someone will come escort you to your table."

"Thanks."

She entered the huge lounge that had beautiful rosettes hanging from the ceiling and several masquerade props in the corners of the room for picture taking. Flamenco dancers encouraged participation in the middle of the floor and several men dressed as dashing bullfighters walked around as servers. When a woman wearing a gorgeous *quinceañcra* gown offered her a beautiful lace fan, Jillian smiled and took it.

"Would the senorita like a glass of rioja?"

"Yes, thanks," she responded to one of the servers.

Jillian took a sip and immediately liked the taste. It wasn't too tart or tangy but was an excellent blend of fruits. As she sipped her wine she looked around the room. It was crowded and most of the individuals were coupled off. Immediately, she felt like a loner crashing a party, but forced the feeling away. So what if there were a lot of couples and she had no one? She'd known it would be like this but had made the decision to come anyway.

"Excuse me, senorita, but someone asked me to give you this," the woman wearing the *quinceañera* gown said, while handing her a single red rose.

"Who?" Jillian asked, curiously glancing around.

The woman smiled. "A *very* handsome man." And then she walked off.

Jillian felt uneasy. What kind of *very* handsome man would come cruising alone? She'd seen a movie once where a serial killer had come on a cruise ship and stalked single women. No one had known just how many women he'd killed and thrown overboard until the end of the cruise. For crying out loud, why was she remembering that particular movie now?

She drew in a deep breath knowing she was letting her imagination get the best of her. The man was probably someone who'd seen her alone and wanted to state his interest by giving her a rose. Romantic but a total waste of his time. Even the woman's claim that he was *very* handsome did nothing for Jillian since she wasn't ready to get involved with anyone. Even after a full year, she compared every man to Aidan. That was the main reason she hadn't dated anyone since him. On the other hand, she would bet any amount of money Aidan was dating someone and probably hadn't wasted any time doing so.

She drew in a deep breath, refusing to let her mind go there. Why should she care in the least what Aidan was doing or who he was doing it with? Deciding not to think of an answer for that one, she glanced around the room, curiosity getting the best of her. She tried to find any single men but all she saw were the bullfighters serving drinks.

Jillian glanced at her watch. She'd deliberately arrived a little late so she wouldn't have long to wait for dinner. She'd grabbed breakfast on the run to catch her plane and because she'd come straight from the Barcelona airport to the ship, she had missed lunch altogether.

After taking another sip of her wine, she was about to check her watch again when suddenly her skin heated. Was that desire floating in her stomach. Why? And for who? This was definitely odd.

Jillian searched the room in earnest as a quiver inched up her spine. Declining a server's offer of another drink, she nearly dismissed what was happening as a figment of her imagination when she saw him. A man wearing a teal-feathered mask stood alone on the other side of the room, watching her. So she watched back, letting her gaze roam over him. Was he the one who'd given her the rose? Who was he? Why was she reacting to him this way?

As she studied him she found him oddly familiar. Was she comparing the man to Aidan to the point where everything about him reminded her of her ex? His height? His build? The low cut of his hair?

She shook her head. She was losing it. She needed another drink after all. That's when the man began walking toward her. She wasn't going crazy. She didn't know the when, how or why of it, but there was no doubt in her mind that the man walking toward her—mask or no mask—was Aidan. No other man had a walk like he did. And those broad shoulders...

He was sex appeal on legs and he walked the part. It was a stroll of self-confidence and sinful eroticism. How could he have this effect on her after a full year? She drew in a deep breath. That's not the question she should be asking. What she wanted to know was why he was on the same cruise with her? She refused to believe it was a coincidence.

Her spine stiffened when he came to a stop in front of her. Her nostrils had picked up his scent from five feet away and now her entire body was responding. Sharp, crackling energy stirred to life between them. And from the look in his eyes he felt it, as well. Hot. Raw. Primal.

She didn't want it. Nor did she need that sort of sexual attraction to him again. She blew out a frustrated breath. "Aidan, what are you doing here?"

* * *

Aidan wasn't surprised that she had recognized him with the mask on. After all, they'd shared a bed for three solid years so she should know him inside out, clothes or not…just like he knew her. Case in point, he knew exactly what she was wearing beneath that clingy black dress. As little as possible, which meant only a bra and thong. And more than likely both were made of lace. She had the figure to handle just about anything she put on— or nothing at all. Frankly, he preferred nothing at all.

"I asked you what you're doing here."

He noted her voice had tightened in anger and he figured it best to answer. "I've always wanted to take a Mediterranean cruise."

She rolled her eyes. "And you want me to believe you being here is a coincidence? That you had no idea I was here on this cruise ship?"

"That's not what I'm saying."

"Then what *are* you saying, Aidan?"

He placed his half-empty wineglass on the tray of a passing waiter, just in case Jillian was tempted to douse him with it. "I'll tell you after dinner."

"After dinner? No, you will tell me *now*."

Her voice had risen and several people glanced over at them. "I think we need to step outside to finish our discussion."

She frowned. "I think not. You can tell me what I want to know right here."

In anger, she walked into the scant space separating them and leaned in close, her lips almost brushing his. That was too close. His bottom lip tingled and his heart beat like crazy when he remembered her taste. A taste he'd become addicted to. A taste he'd gone a year without.

"I wouldn't bring my mouth any closer if I were you," he warned in a rough whisper.

She blinked as if realizing how close they were. Heeding his warning, she quickly took a step back. "I still want answers, Aidan. What are you doing here?"

He decided to be totally honest with her. Give her the naked truth and let her deal with it. "I came on this cruise, Jillian, with the full intention of winning you back."

Eleven

Jillian stared at Aidan as his words sank in. That's when she decided it would be best for them to take this discussion to a more private area after all. She removed her mask. "I think we need to step outside the room, Aidan."

When they stepped into a vacant hallway, she turned to him. "How dare you assume all you had to do was follow me on this cruise to win me back?"

He pulled off his mask and she fought back a jolt of desire when she looked into his face. How could any man get more handsome in a year's time? Yes, she'd seen him a couple of times since their break-up, but she had avoided getting this close to him. He appeared to have gotten an inch or so taller, his frame was even more muscular and his looks were twice as gorgeous.

"I have given it some thought," he said, leaning back against a railing.

"Evidently, not enough," she countered, not liking how her gaze, with a mind of its own, was traveling over him. He was wearing a dark suit, and he looked like a male model getting ready for a photo shoot—immaculate with nothing out of place.

"Evidently, you've forgotten one major thing about me," she said.

"What? Just how stubborn you are?" he asked, smiling, as if trying to make light of her anger, which irritated her even more.

"That, too, but also that once I make up my mind about something, that's it. And I made up my mind that my life can sail a lot more calmly without you." She watched his expression to see if her words had any effect, but she couldn't tell if they had.

He studied her in silence before saying, "Sorry you feel that way, Jillian. But I intend to prove you wrong."

She lifted a brow. "Excuse me?"

"Over the next fourteen days I intend to prove that your life can't sail more calmly without me. In fact, I intend to show you that you don't even like calm. You need turbulence, furor and even a little mayhem."

She shook her head. "If you believe that then you truly don't know me at all."

"I know you. I also know the real reason you broke things off with me. Why didn't you tell me what you *thought* you saw in my apartment the night of my birthday party?"

She wondered how he'd found out about that. It really didn't matter at this point. "It's not what I *thought* I saw, Aidan. It's what I saw. A woman giving you a lap dance, which you seemed to enjoy, before she began stripping off her clothes." Saying it made the memory flash in her mind and roused her anger that much more.

"She was a paid entertainer, Jillian. All the ladies there that night were. Several of my frat brothers thought I'd been living a boring and dull life and decided to add some excitement into it. I admit they might have gone a little overboard."

"And you enjoyed every minute of it."

He shrugged. "I had a few drinks and—"

"You don't know what all you did, do you?"

He frowned. "I remember fine. Other than the lap dance and her strip act...and a couple other women stripping...nothing else happened."

"Wasn't that enough?" she asked, irritated that he thought several naked women on display in his apartment were of little significance. "And why didn't you tell me about the party? You led me to believe you'd done just as you said you were going to do—watch TV and go to bed."

He released a deep breath. "Okay, I admit I should have told you and I was wrong for not doing so. But I was angry with you. It was my birthday and I wanted to spend it with you. I felt you could have sacrificed a little that weekend to be with me. I hadn't known you changed your mind and flew to Portland."

He paused a moment and then continued, "I realized after we'd broken up just how unpleasant my attitude had been and I do apologize for that. I was getting frustrated with the secrecy surrounding our affair, with my work and how little time I could get off to fly to New Orleans to spend with you."

As far as Jillian was concerned, his attitude had been more than unpleasant; it had become downright unacceptable. He wasn't the only one who'd been frustrated with their situation. She had, too, which was the reason she had decided to confess all to Pam.

"Now that you're finished with medical school, there's no reason to keep our secret any longer anyway," he said, interrupting her thoughts.

She frowned. "And I see no reason to reveal it. Ever," she said. "Especially in light of one very important fact."

"And what fact is that?"

"The fact that we aren't together and we won't ever be together again."

If she figured that then she was wrong.

They *would* be together again. He was counting on it. It was the reason he'd come on the cruise. The one thing she had not said was that she no longer loved him. And as long as she had feelings for him then he could accomplish anything. At this point, even if she claimed she didn't love him, he would have to prove her wrong because he believed she loved him just as much as he loved her. Their relationship was just going through a few hiccups, which he felt they could resolve.

"If you truly believe that then you have nothing to worry about," he said.

She frowned. "Meaning what?"

"Meaning my presence on this ship shouldn't bother you."

She lifted her chin. "It won't unless you become a nuisance."

A smile spread across his face. "Nuisance? I think not. But I do intend to win you back, like I said. Then we can move on with our lives. I see marriage and babies in our future."

She laughed. "You've got to be kidding. Didn't you hear what I said? We won't be getting back together, so we don't have a future."

"And you're willing to throw away the last three years?"

"What I've done is make it easy for you."

He lifted a brow. "To do what?"

"Go back to your womanizing ways. You seemed to

be enjoying yourself so much at your birthday party I wouldn't think of denying you the opportunity."

He crossed his arms over his chest. "I gave up my so-called womanizing ways when I fell in love with you."

"Could have fooled me with your lap dancer and all those strippers waiting their turn."

"Like I said, I didn't invite them."

"But you could have asked them to leave."

He shrugged. "Yes, I could have. But you're going to have to learn to trust me, Jillian. I can see where my attitude leading up to that night might have been less than desirable, but at no time have I betrayed you with another woman. Do you intend to punish me forever for one night of a little fun?"

"I'm not punishing you, Aidan. I'm not doing anything to you. I didn't invite you on this cruise. You took it upon yourself to…"

Her words trailed off and she gazed at him suspiciously before saying, "Paige and I were supposed to go on this cruise together and she had to back out when she had a conflict, which is why I came alone. Please tell me you had nothing to do with that."

He'd known she would eventually figure things out but he had hoped it wouldn't be this soon. "Okay, I won't tell you."

She was back in his face again. "You told Paige about us? Now she knows I was duped by a womanizer."

Her lips were mere inches from his again. Evidently, she'd forgotten his earlier warning. "I am not a womanizer, and I didn't tell her anything about us. She figured things out on her own. Ivy told Paige about the lap dance and Paige told me. And I appreciate her doing so."

From Jill's expression he could tell that although he

might appreciate it, she didn't. "I am so upset with you, right now, Aidan. You are—"

Suddenly he pulled her into his arms. "You were warned."

Then he captured her mouth with his.

Push him away. Push him away. Push him away, a voice inside of Jillian's head chanted.

But her body would not obey. Instead of pushing him away, she leaned in closer, wrapping her arms around his neck.

Had it been a year since she had enjoyed this? A year since she'd had the taste of his tongue inside her mouth? Doing all those crazy things in every nook and cranny? Making liquid heat she'd held at bay shoot straight to the area between her legs?

How could any woman deal with a master kisser like him? She would admit that during the past year she had gone to bed dreaming of this but the real thing surpassed any dream she'd ever had.

The sound of voices made them pull apart. She drew in a deep breath, turning her back to him so she could lick her lips without him seeing her do so. That had been one hell of a kiss. Her lips were still electrified.

She turned back around and caught him tracing his tongue across his own lips. Her stomach clenched. "I think you have it all wrong, Aidan," she managed to say.

"After that kiss, I'd say I got it all right."

"Think whatever you like," she said, walking away.

"Hey, where're you going? The Madrid Room is this way."

She stopped and turned. "I'll order room service."

Jillian continued walking, feeling the heat of his gaze on her back.

Aidan watched her walk away, appreciating the sway of her hips. He drew in a deep breath. He loved the woman. If there was any doubt in her mind of that—which there seemed to be—he would wipe it out.

Turning, he headed toward his own cabin, thinking room service sounded pretty good. Besides, he had shocked Jillian's senses enough for today. Tomorrow he planned to lay it on even thicker. She had warned him not to be a nuisance. He smiled at the thought. He wouldn't be a nuisance, just totally effective.

Tonight they had talked, although he seemed to annoy her and he'd found her somewhat infuriating. But at least they knew where they both stood. She knew he was aware of the real reason she'd ended things between them. He had to convince her that his life as a womanizer was definitely behind him, that he had no desire to return to that life again.

He would admit getting rid of the lap dancer that night hadn't been easy. Somehow she'd figured it would be okay to hang around after the party was over. She'd been quick to let him know there wouldn't be an overtime charge. He had countered, letting her know he wasn't interested.

When Aidan reached his suite, he saw the elephant made of hand towels on his bed. Cute. But not as cute as the woman he intended to have back in his arms.

Jillian checked the time as she made a call to Paige. It was around ten in the morning in L.A., so there was no reason her sister shouldn't answer the phone. Paige was definitely going to get an earful from her.

"Why are you calling me? Aren't rates higher on the high seas?" Paige asked, answering on the fourth ring.

Jillian frowned. "Don't worry about the cost of the rates. Why didn't you tell me you knew about me and Aidan?"

"Why hadn't you told *me* so I wouldn't have to tell you? And don't say because it was supposed to be a secret."

"Well, it was. How did you figure it out?"

"Wasn't hard to do. Both of you started getting sloppy with it. Aidan slipped and called you Jilly a couple of times, and I caught you almost drooling whenever he walked into the room."

"I did not."

"You did, too. Besides, I knew you had a crush on him that first time we met the Westmoreland family at Pam's engagement party. You kept me up all night asking, 'Isn't Aidan cute, Paige? Isn't he cute?'"

Jillian smiled as she remembered. She had been so taken with Aidan. Although he and Adrian were identical twins it had been Aidan who pushed her buttons. "Well, no thanks to you he's here and he wants me back."

"Do you want him to get you back?"

"No. You didn't see that lap dance. I did."

"Didn't have to see it because I've seen one before. I know they can get rather raunchy. But it was a birthday party. His. Thrown by his friends and the lap dancer and the strippers were entertainment."

"Some entertainment," she mumbled. "He enjoyed it. You should have seen the look on his face when the woman shoved her girls at him."

"Pleeze. He's a man. They enjoy seeing a pair of

breasts. Anytime or anyplace. Will it make you feel better if I get the Chippendales dancers for your next birthday party?"

"This isn't funny, Paige."

"You don't hear me laughing. If anything, you should hear me moaning. Can you imagine a lap dance from one of those guys? If you can't, I can. And my imagination is running pretty wild right now."

Jillian shook her head. "Before I let you go, there's one more thing. Did you really get a part in a Spielberg movie?"

"No."

"So you lied."

"I was acting, and I evidently did a great job. It sounds like you have some serious decisions to make about Aidan. But don't rush. You have fourteen days. In the meantime, enjoy the cruise. Enjoy life. Enjoy Aidan. He plans on getting you back. I'd like to be there to watch him try. I've got my money on him, by the way."

"Sounds like you have money to lose. Goodbye, Paige." Jillian clicked off the phone, refusing to let her sister get in the last word, especially if it would be a word she really didn't want to hear.

Regardless of what Paige said, her sister hadn't been there to witness that lap dance. She hadn't seen that salacious grin on Aidan's face while looking up at the half-naked woman sprawled all over him. There was no doubt in Jillian's mind that he'd enjoyed every minute of it. He had wanted those women there; otherwise, he would have asked them and his friends to leave. And although he claimed otherwise, how could she be certain one of those women didn't spend the night with him; especially since he didn't tell Jillian anything about the party, even when she had asked? She of all people knew what a healthy sexual appetite Aidan had, and they hadn't seen each other in more than three months. And at the time, that had been the longest amount of time they'd been apart.

Before getting in bed later that night, Jillian checked the ship's agenda. Tomorrow was a full day at sea and she refused to stay locked in her cabin. This was a big ship and chances were she might not run into Aidan. She knew the odds of that were slim; especially when he admitted his only reason for coming on the cruise was to win her back. Well, he could certainly try.

She could not deny it had felt good to be kissed by him tonight. Pretty damn good. But there was more to any relationship than kisses. Even the hot, raw, carnal kind that Aidan gave. And when he took a mind to kiss her all over…

She drew in a deep breath, refusing to let her thoughts go there. He would probably try using his sexual wiles to win her back. And she intended to be ready to disappoint him.

Twelve

"Good morning, Jillian."

Jillian glanced up from the book she was reading to watch Aidan slide onto the lounger beside her. She was on the upper deck near the pool. Why had she thought he would never find her here?

"Good morning," she grumbled and went back to her reading. Although she had gone to bed fairly early, she hadn't gotten a good night's sleep. The man stretched on the lounger beside her had invaded her dreams not once or twice, but all through the night.

"Had breakfast yet?"

She glanced away from her book to look over at him. "Yes." She remembered the pancakes and syrup she'd enjoyed. "It was tasty."

"Um, bet it wasn't tasty as you. Want to go back to my cabin and be my breakfast?"

His question caused a spark of heat to settle between her thighs. Something she definitely didn't need after all those erotic dreams she'd had. "You shouldn't say something like that to me."

"You prefer I say it to someone else?"

She narrowed her gaze. "Do whatever you want. At breakfast I happened to notice a group of women on the cruise. All appeared single. I think I overheard one say they're part of some book club."

"You want me to go check out other women?"

"Won't matter to me. Need I remind you that we aren't together?"

"And need I remind you that I'm working on that? And by the way, I have a proposition for you."

"Whatever it is, the answer is no."

He chuckled. "You haven't heard it."

"Doesn't matter."

"You certain?"

"Positive."

He smiled over at her. "Okay then. I'm glad. In fact, you've made my day by not accepting it. I'm happy that you turned it down."

She stared over at him and frowned. "Really? And just what was this proposition?"

In a warm, teasing tone, he said. "I thought you didn't want to hear it."

"I've changed my mind."

He nodded. "I guess I can allow you to do that." He shifted and sat up. She tried not to notice the khaki shorts he wore and how well they fit the lower half of his body. Or how his muscle shirt covered perfect abs.

He took her hand, easing her into the same sitting position he was in, as if what he had to say was something he didn't want others around them to overhear.

"Well?" she asked, trying to ignore the tingling sensation in the hand he touched.

"You're aware the only reason I came on this cruise was to get you back, right?"

She shrugged. "So you say."

A smile touched the corners of his lips. "Well, I

thought about a few of the things you said last night and I wanted to offer you a chance to make some decisions."

She lifted a brow. "Like what?"

"Like whether or not I should even pursue you at all. I don't want to be that nuisance you insinuated I could be. So my proposition was that I just leave you alone and wait patiently for you to come to me. I hope you know what that means since you just turned it down."

She would not have turned it down had she heard him out, and he knew it. Unfortunately, she could guess what the consequences would be and she had a feeling she wasn't going to like it. "What does that mean, Aidan?"

He leaned in closer to whisper in her ear. His warm breath felt like a soft, sensuous lick across her skin. "I want you so bad, Jillian, that I ache. And that means I'm not giving up until you're back in my bed."

She immediately felt a pounding pulse at the tips of her breasts. She leaned back to stare at him and the razor-sharp sensuality openly displayed in his gaze almost made her moan.

"And before you ask, Jillian, the answer is no. It isn't just about sex with me," he murmured in a low, husky tone. "It's about me wanting the woman I love both mentally and physically. You're constantly in my mind but physically, it's been over a year."

She drew in a deep breath and felt the essence of what he'd said in every single nerve ending in her body. It had been over a year. With Aidan she'd had a pretty active sex life, and although there were periods of time when they were apart, they always made up for any time lost whenever they were together.

"Your needing sex is not my problem," she finally said.

"Isn't it?" he countered. "Can you look me in the eyes

and say that you don't want me as much as I want you? That you didn't dream about us making love last night? Me being inside you. You riding me? Hard. My tongue inside your mouth…and inside a lot of other places on your body?"

She silently stared at him but her entire body flared in response to the vivid pictures he'd painted in her mind. Unlike Paige, Jillian wasn't an actress and couldn't lie worth a damn. But on that same note she would never admit anything to him. That would give him too much power. "I won't admit to anything, Aidan."

"You don't have to," he said, with a serious smile on his face. "And it's not about me needing sex but me needing you." He paused a moment as if giving his words time to sink in. "But this leads to another proposition I'd like to make."

She'd set herself up for this one. "And what is the proposition this time?"

He leaned in closer. "That for the remainder of the cruise you let your guard down. Believe in me. Believe in yourself. And believe in us. I want you to see I'm still the man who loves you. The man who will always love you. But that's something you have to believe, Jillian. However, at the end of the cruise, if for whatever reason, you still don't believe it or feel that the two of us can make a lifetime commitment, then when we dock back in Barcelona, we'll agree to go our separate ways."

She broke eye contact with him to glance out at the ocean. Today was a rather calm day outside but inside she was in a state of turmoil. He was asking a lot of her and he knew it. His proposition meant forgetting the very reason she broke up with him. That would definitely be easy on him if she did. Was that why he'd come up with this latest proposition?

Jillian turned her gaze back to him. "You want me to just forget everything that's happened, Aidan? Especially the incident that caused our breakup?"

"No, I don't want you to forget a single thing."

His answer surprised her. "Why?"

"Because it's important that the two of us learn from any mistakes we've made, and we can't do that if we safely tuck them away just because doing so will be convenient. We should talk about them openly and honestly. Hopefully, we'll be able to build something positive out of the discussions. You're always harping a lot on the things I did. What about you, Jillian? Do you think you were completely blameless?"

"No, but—"

"I don't want to get into all that now, but have you ever noticed that with you there's always a *but* in there somewhere?"

She frowned at him. "No, I never noticed but obviously you have." Was it really that way with her? As far as sharing the blame, she could do that. But she hadn't been the one getting a lap dance.

"My proposition is still on the table," he said. "I've been completely honest with you on this cruise, Jillian. I've been up-front with my intentions, my wants and my desires."

Yes, he had. Every opportunity he got. And she knew that he would have her on her back in a flash if she were to let him. Jillian inclined her head to look deeper into his eyes. "And you promise that at the end of the cruise if things don't work out the way we think they should that you will go your way and I'll go mine?"

He nodded slowly. "It would be difficult, but yes. I want you to be happy and if being happy for you means not having me in your life then that's the way it will be. It will be your decision and I would like to have that decision the night before we return to Barcelona."

She digested what Aidan said. He'd laid things out, with no fluff. She knew what, and who, she would be dealing with. But she also knew that even if she decided she didn't want him in her life romantically, he could never be fully out of it; their families were connected. How could they manage that?

"What about the family?" she asked. "Paige, Stern and Adrian know our secret. If things don't work out between us it might have an effect on them."

"We will deal with that if it happens. Together. Even if we're no longer lovers, there's no reason we can't remain friends. Besides, are you sure there aren't others in the family besides those three who know? It's my guess others might suspect something even if they haven't said anything."

She shrugged. "Doesn't matter who knows now. I had planned on telling Pam anyway."

Surprise flashed in his eyes. "You had?"

"Yes."

"When?"

"After I talked to you about it, which I had planned to do when I flew into Portland for your birthday."

"Oh."

She released a sigh. Evidently the one thing he hadn't found out was that she'd intended to release him from their secret. "Afterward, when things didn't work out between us, I saw no need for me to tell Pam anything.

In fact, I felt the less she knew about the situation, the better."

Aidan didn't say anything for a moment and neither did Jillian. She figured he was thinking how that one weekend had changed things for them. He finally broke the silence by asking, "So, what's your answer to my proposition?"

Jillian nibbled at her bottom lip. Why couldn't she just turn him down, walk away and keep walking? She knew one of the reasons was that her mind was filled with fond memories of the good times they'd shared. It hadn't been all bad.

Would it be so dreadful if she were to give his proposition a try? What did she have to lose? She'd already experienced heartbreak with him. And a year of separation hadn't been easy. Besides, she couldn't deny that it would feel good to be with him out in the open, without any kind of secrecy shrouding them. Whenever he'd come to Laramie, she'd always been on guard, looking over her shoulder in case she ran into someone who knew Pam. And he did have a good point about the remaining days on the cruise testing the strength of a relationship between them.

She met his gaze. "Yes. I accept your proposition and I will hold you to your word, Aidan."

Later that night, as Aidan changed for dinner, he couldn't help remembering Jillian's words.

"Fine, baby, hold me to my word," he murmured to himself as he tucked his white dress shirt into his pants. "That's the way it should be. And that's the way it will be."

Today had gone just the way he'd wanted. After she'd

agreed to his proposition he'd been able to talk her into going with him to the Terelle Deck so he could grab breakfast. She'd sat across from him while he ate a hefty portion of the pancakes and syrup she'd recommended. They had chosen a table with a beautiful view of the ocean, and he liked the way the cool morning breeze stirred her hair. More than once he'd been tempted to reach across the table and run his fingers through it.

After breakfast he had talked her into joining him in the Venus Lounge where a massive bingo game was under way. They had found a table in the back and she'd worked five bingo cards while he worked three. In the end, neither of them had won anything but the game had been fun.

Later they had gone to the art gallery to check out the paintings on display and after that they'd enjoyed a delicious lunch in the Coppeneria Room. After she mentioned her plans to visit the spa, he'd taken a stroll around the ship. The layout was awesome and the entire ship was gorgeous. Tomorrow morning before daybreak they would arrive in Monte Carlo, France, and from there, Florence, Italy. He'd never been to France or Italy before but Adrian had, and according to his twin both countries were beautiful. Aidan couldn't wait to see them for himself.

He smiled as he put on his cuff links. Being around Jillian today had reminded him of how much she liked having her way. In the past he had indulged her. But not this time. While on this cruise he had no intention of letting her have her way. In fact, he planned to teach her the art of compromising. That was the main reason he had suggested she drop by his cabin to grab him for dinner instead of the other way around. Although she hadn't said anything, he could tell she hadn't liked the idea.

He turned from the mirror at the sound of a knock on his door. She was a little early but he had no problem with that. Moving across the suite, he opened the door, and then stood there, finding it impossible to speak. All he could do was stare at Jillian. Dressed in a red floor-length gown that hugged every curve, her hair wrapped on top of her head with a few curls dangling toward her beautiful face, she looked breathtaking. His gaze scanned the length of her—head to toe.

Pulling himself together, he stepped aside. "Come in. You look very nice."

"Thank you," she said, entering his suite. "I'm a little early. The cabin steward arrived and I didn't want to get in his way."

"No problem. I just need to put on my tie."

"This suite is fantastic. I thought my suite was large but this one is triple mine in size."

He smiled over at her. "It's the owner's personal suite whenever he cruises."

"Really? And how did you get so lucky?"

"He's a friend. You remember my cousin Quade who lives in North Carolina, right?"

"The one who has the triplets?"

"Yes, he's the one. Quade and the ship's owner, Dominic Saxon, are brothers-in-law, married to sisters—the former Steeles, Cheyenne and Taylor.

Jillian nodded. "I remember meeting Cheyenne at Dillon and Pam's wedding. The triplets were adorable. I don't recall ever meeting Taylor."

"I'll make sure you meet Taylor and Dominic if you ever come to visit me in Charlotte." He'd deliberately chosen his words to make sure she understood that if a meeting took place, it would be her decision.

After putting on his tie, he turned to her, trying not to stare again. "I'm all set. Ready?"

"Whenever you are."

He was tempted to kiss her but held back. Knowing him like she did, she would probably expect such a move. But tonight he planned to keep her on her toes. In other words, he would be full of surprises.

"Hi, Aidan!"

Jillian figured it would be one of those nights when the group of women sharing their table chorused the greeting to Aidan. It was the book-club group. She should have known they would find him. Or, for all she knew, he'd found them.

"I take it you've met them," she whispered when he pulled out her chair.

"Yes, earlier today, while taking my stroll when you were at the spa."

"Evening, ladies. How's everyone doing?" Aidan asked the group with familiarity, taking his seat.

"Fine," they responded simultaneously. Jillian noticed some were smiling so hard it made her wonder how any-one's lips could stretch that wide.

"I want you all to meet someone," Aidan was saying. "This is Jillian Novak. My significant other."

"Oh."

Was that disappointment she heard in the voices of the six women? And what happened to those huge smiles? Well, she would just have to show them how it was done. She smiled brightly and then said, "Hello, everyone."

Only a few returned her greeting, but she didn't care because she was reflecting on Aidan's introduction.

My significant other.

Before their breakup they had been together for three years and this was the first time he'd introduced her to anyone because of their secret. It made her realize that, other than Ivy, she'd never introduced him to anyone, either.

The waiter came to take their order but not before giving them a run-down of all the delectable meals on the menu tonight. Jillian chose a seafood dinner and Aidan selected steak.

She discreetly checked out the six women engaging in conversation with Aidan. All beautiful. Gorgeously dressed. Articulate. Professional. Single.

"So, how long have the two of you been together?" asked one of the women who'd introduced herself earlier as Wanda.

Since it appeared the woman had directed the question to Aidan, Jillian let him answer. "Four years," he said, spreading butter on his bread. Jillian decided not to remind him that one of those years they hadn't been together.

"Four years? Really?" a woman by the name of Sandra asked, extending her lips into what Jillian could tell was a plastered-on smile.

"Yes, *really*," Jillian responded, knowing just what the chick was getting at. After four years Jillian should have a ring on her finger. In other words, she should be a wife and not a significant other.

"Then I guess the two of you will probably be tying the knot pretty soon." It was obvious Wanda was dig-

ging for information. The others' ears were perked up
as if they, too, couldn't wait to hear the response.

Jillian tried not to show her surprise when Aidan
reached across the table and placed his hand over hers.
"Sooner rather than later, if I had my way. But I'll be
joining the Cardiology Department at Johns Hopkins in
the fall, and Jillian's just finished medical school, so we
haven't set dates yet."

"You're both doctors?" Sandra asked, smiling.

"Yes," both Aidan and Jillian answered at the same
time.

"That's great. So are we," Sandra said, pointing to
herself and the others. "Faye and Sherri and I just finished Meharry Medical School a couple of months ago,
and Wanda, Joy and Virginia just completed pharmacy
school at Florida A&M."

"Congratulations, everyone," Jillian said, giving all
six women a genuine smile. After having completed
medical school she knew the hard work and dedication
that was required for any medical field. And the six had
definitely attended excellent schools.

"And congratulations to you, too," the women said
simultaneously.

Jillian's smile widened. "Thanks."

Aidan glanced down at the woman walking beside
him as they left the jazz lounge where several musicians
had performed. Jillian had been pretty quiet since dinner. He couldn't help wondering what she was thinking.

"Did you enjoy dinner?" he asked.

She glanced up at him. "Yes, what about you?"

He shrugged. "It was nice."

"Just nice? You were the only male seated at a table

with several females, all gorgeous, so how was it just nice?"

"Because it was," he said, wondering if this conversation would start a discussion he'd rather not have with her. But then, maybe they should have it now. They *had* agreed to talk things out. "So what did you think of the ladies at our table tonight?"

She stopped walking to lean against a rail and look at him. "Maybe I should be asking what you thought of them."

He joined her at the rail, standing a scant foot in front of her. "Pretty. All seven of them. But the prettiest of them all was the one wearing the red dress. The one named Jillian Novak. Now, she was a total knockout. She put the *s* in sexy."

Jillian smiled and shook her head, sending those dangling curls swinging. "Laying it on rather thick, aren't you, Aidan?"

"Not as long as you get the picture."

"And what picture is that?"

"That you're the only woman I want. The only one who can get blood rushing through my veins."

She chuckled. "Sounds serious, Dr. Westmoreland."

"It is." He didn't say anything for a minute as he stared at her. "Do you realize that this is the first time you've ever referred to me as Dr. Westmoreland?"

She nodded. "Yes, I know. Just like I realized tonight at dinner that it was the first time you'd ever introduced me during the time we were together."

"Yes. There were times when I wished I could have."

But you couldn't, she thought. *Because of the secret I made you keep.*

"But I did tonight."

"Yes, you did fib a little. Twice in fact," she pointed out.

He lifted a brow. "When?"

"When you said I was your significant other."

"I didn't fib. You are. There's no one more significant in my life than you," he said softly.

Jillian couldn't say anything after that. How could she? And when the silence between them lengthened, she wondered if he was expecting her to respond. What *could* she say? That she believed him? Did she really?

"And what was the other?" he asked, finally breaking the silence.

"What other?" she asked him.

"Fib. You said there were two."

"Oh. The one about the amount of time we've been together. You said four years and it was three," she said as they began walking again.

"No, it was four. Although we spent a year apart it meant nothing to me, other than frustration and anger. Nevertheless, you were still here," he said, touching his heart. "During every waking moment and in all my dreams."

She glanced away from him as they continued walking only to glance back moments later. "That sounds unfair to the others."

"What others?"

"Any woman you dated that year."

He stopped walking, took her hand and pulled her to the side, back over to the rail. He frowned down at her. "What are you talking about? I didn't date any women last year."

She searched his face and somehow saw the truth

in his words. "But why? I thought you would. Figured you had."

"Why?" Before she could respond he went on in a mocking tone, "Ah, that's right. Because I'm a womanizer."

Jillian heard the anger in his voice, but yes, that was the reason she'd thought he'd dated. Wasn't that the reason she had ended things between them as well, so he would have the freedom to return to his old ways? She drew in a deep breath. "Aidan, I—"

"No, don't say it." He stiffened his chin. "Whatever it is you're going to say, Jillian, don't." He glanced down at his watch and then his gaze moved back to her face. "I know you prefer turning in early, so I'll see you back to your cabin. I think I'll hang out a while in one of the bars."

She didn't say anything for a moment. "Want some company?"

"No," he said softly. "Not right now."

Suddenly, she felt a deep ache in her chest. "Okay. Don't worry about seeing me to my cabin. You can go on."

"You sure?"

She forced a smile. "Yes, I'm sure. I know the way."

"All right. I'll come get you for breakfast around eight."

If you can still stand my company, she thought. "Okay. I'll see you in the morning at eight."

He nodded and, with the hurt she'd brought on herself eating away at her, she watched Aidan walk away.

Thirteen

Aidan forced his eyes open when he heard banging coming from the sitting area.

"What the hell?" He closed his eyes as sharp pain slammed through his head. It was then that he remembered last night. Every single detail.

He had stopped at the bar, noticed it was extremely crowded and had gone to his room instead. He'd ordered room service, a bottle of his favorite Scotch. He'd sat on the balcony, looking out over the ocean beneath the night sky and drinking alone, nursing a bruised heart. He didn't finish off the entire bottle but he'd downed enough to give him the mother of all headaches this morning. What time was it anyway?

He forced his eyes back open to look at the clock on the nightstand. Ten? It was ten in the morning? Crap! He'd promised Jillian to take her to breakfast at eight. He could only imagine what she'd thought when he was a no-show. Pulling himself up on the side of the bed he drew in a deep breath. Honestly, did he care anymore? She had him pegged as a player in that untrusting mind of hers, so what did the truth matter?

"Mr. Aidan," called the cabin steward, "do you want me to clean your bedroom now or come back later?"

"Come back later, Rowan."

When Aidan heard the door close, he dropped back in bed. He knew he should call Jillian, but chances were she'd gotten tired of waiting around and had gone to breakfast without him. He could imagine her sitting there eating pancakes while all kinds of insane ideas flowed through her head. All about him. Hell, he might as well get up, get dressed and search the ship for her to put those crazy ideas to rest.

He was about to get out of bed when he heard a knock at the door. He figured it was probably the guy coming around to pick up laundry, so he slipped into his pajama bottoms to tell the person to come back later.

He snatched open the door but instead of the laundry guy, Jillian stood there carrying a tray of food. "Jillian? What are you doing here?"

She stared at him for a moment. "You look like crap."

"I feel like crap," he muttered, moving aside to let her in. She placed the tray on his dining table. His head still pounded somewhat, but not as hard as the way his erection throbbed while staring at her. She was wearing a cute and sexy shorts set that showed what a gorgeous pair of legs she had. And her hair, which had been pinned atop her head last night, flowed down her shoulders while gold hoop earrings dangled from her ears. Damn, he couldn't handle this much sexiness in the morning.

She turned around. "To answer your question as to why I'm here, you missed breakfast so I thought I'd bring you something to eat."

He closed the door and leaned against it. "And what else?"

She lifted a brow. "And what else?"

"Yes. What other reason do you have for coming here? Let me guess. You figured I brought a woman here last night and you wanted to catch me in the act? Right? Go ahead, Jillian, search my bedroom if you like. The bathroom, too, if that suits your fancy. Oh, and don't forget to check the balconies in case I've hidden her out there until after you leave."

Jillian didn't say anything for a long minute. "I guess I deserved that. But—"

He held his hand to interrupt her. "Please. No buts, Jillian. I'm tired of them coming from you. Let me ask you something. How many men did you sleep with during the year we weren't together since you think I didn't leave a single woman standing?"

She narrowed her gaze at him. "Not a single one."

He crossed his arms over his chest. "Why?"

She lifted a chin. "Because I didn't want to."

"Why didn't you want to? You had broken things off with me and we weren't together. Why didn't you sleep with another man?"

Jillian knew she'd screwed up badly last night and she could hardly wait until morning to see Aidan so she could apologize. When he didn't show up at eight as he'd promised, she would admit that for a quick second she'd thought he might have been mad enough to spend the night with someone else. But all it had taken to erase that thought was for her to remember how he'd looked last night when he told her the reason why he'd introduced her as his significant other.

There's no one more significant in my life than you. And she believed him. His reason for not sleeping with another woman during the year they'd been apart was the same reason she hadn't slept with another man.

"Jillian?"

She met his gaze. He wanted an answer and she would give him one. The truth and nothing but the truth.

"Sleeping with another man never crossed my mind, Aidan," she said softly. "Because I still loved you. And no matter what I saw or imagined you did with that lap dancer, I still loved you. My body has your imprint all over it and the thought of another man touching it sickens me."

She paused and then added, "You're wrong. I didn't come here thinking I'd find another woman. I came to apologize. I figured the reason you didn't come take me to breakfast was because you were still mad at me. And after last night I knew that I deserved your anger."

"Why do you think you deserve my anger?"

"Because everything is my fault. You only kept our affair a secret because I asked you to, begged you to. Last night when I got to my room, I sat out on the balcony and thought about everything. I forced myself to see the situation through someone else's eyes other than my own. And you know what I saw, Aidan?"

"No, what did you see, Jillian?"

She fought back tears. "I saw a man who loved me enough to take a lot of crap. I never thought about what all the secrecy would mean. And then the long distance and the sacrifices you made to come see me whenever you could. The money you spent for airplane fare, your time. I wasn't the only one with the goal of becoming a doctor. It's not like you didn't have a life, trying to handle the pressure of your dual residency."

She paused. "And I can just imagine what your

friends thought when all of a sudden you became a saint
for no reason. You couldn't tell them about me, so I can
understand them wanting to help get your life back on
track with those women. That was the Aidan they knew.
And unfortunately that was the Aidan I wanted to think
you missed being. That night I showed up at the party,
I should have realized that you were just having the fun
you deserved. Fun you'd denied yourself since your involvement with me. I should have loved you enough and
trusted you enough to believe that no matter what, you
wouldn't betray me. That I meant more to you than any
lap dancer with silicone boobs."

He uncrossed his arms. "You're right. You do mean
more to me than any lap dancer, stripper, book-club
member or any other woman out there, Jillian," he said
in a soft tone. "And you were wrong to think I missed
my old life. What I miss is being with you. I think we
handled things okay that first year, but during those
second and third years, because of trying to make that
dual residency program work and still keep you at the
top of the list, things became difficult for me. Then in
the third year, I was the one with focusing issues. It became harder and harder to keep our long-distance affair
afloat and stay focused at work. And the secrecy only
added more stress. But I knew if I complained to you
about it, that it would only stress you out and make you
lose focus on what you needed to do.

"You were young when we started our affair. Only
twenty-one. And you hadn't dated much. In all honesty, probably not at all, because I refuse to count that
dude you dated in high school. So deep down I knew
you weren't quite ready for the type of relationship I
wanted. But I loved you and I wanted you and I figured

everything would work out. I knew how challenging medical school could be and I wanted to make your life as calm as possible. I didn't want to be the one to add to your stress."

He paused. "But it looks like I did anyway. I tried to make the best of it, but unfortunately sometimes when we talked, I was in one of my foul moods because of stress. I would get an attitude with you instead of talking to you about it. At no time should I have made you feel that you deserved my anger. I apologize. I regret doing that."

"It's okay," Jillian said, pulling out a chair. "Come sit down and eat. Your food is getting cold."

She watched him move away from the door. When he reached the table, she skirted back so he could sit down. When he sat, he reached out, grabbed her around the waist and brought her down to his lap.

"Aidan! What do you think you're doing?"

He wrapped both arms around her so she wouldn't go anywhere. "What I should have done last night. Brought you back here and put you in my lap, wrapped my arms around you and convinced you that I meant everything I said about your value to me. Instead I got upset and walked away."

She pressed her forehead to his and whispered, "Sorry I made you upset with me last night."

"I love you so much, Jillian, and when I think you don't believe just how much I love you, how much you mean to me, I get frustrated and wonder just what else I have to do. I'm not a perfect man. I'm human. I'm going to make mistakes. We both are. But the one thing I won't do is betray your love with another woman. Those days are over for me. You're all the woman I'll ever need."

She leaned back from him to look in his eyes. "I believe you, Aidan. I won't lie and say I'll never get jealous, but I can say it'll be because I'm questioning the woman's motives, not yours."

And she really meant that. When he hadn't come down for breakfast she had gone into the Terelle Dining Room to eat alone. She ran into the book-club ladies and ended up eating breakfast with them and enjoying herself. Once Aidan had made it clear last night that he was not available, they had put a lid on their man-hunter instincts. Jillian and the six women had a lot in common, since they were all recent medical-school graduates, and they enjoyed sharing their experiences over breakfast. They invited her to join them for shopping at some point during their two days in Rome and she agreed to do that.

She shifted in Aidan's lap to find a more comfortable position.

"I wouldn't do that too many times if I were you," he warned in a husky whisper.

A hot wave of desire washed over her. He was looking at her with those dark, penetrating eyes of eyes. The same ones that could arouse her as no man ever had… or would. "Why not?"

If he was going to give her a warning, she wanted him to explain himself, although she knew what he meant.

"Because if you keep it up, *you* might become my breakfast."

The thought of that happening had the muscles between her legs tightening, and she was aware that every hormone in her body was downright sizzling. "But you like pancakes and syrup," she said innocently.

A smile spread across his lips. "But I like your taste better."

"Do you?" she asked, intentionally shifting again to lean forward so that she could bury her face in the hollow of his throat. He was shirtless and she loved getting close to him, drinking in his scent.

"You did it again."

She leaned back and met his gaze. "Did I?"

"Yes."

She intentionally shifted in his lap when she lowered her head to lick the upper part of his chest. She loved the salty taste of his flesh and loved even more the moan she heard from his lips.

"It's been a year, Jillian. If I get you in my bed today it will be a long time before I let you out."

"And miss touring Monte Carlo? The ship has already docked."

"We have time." He suddenly stood, with her in his arms, and she quickly grabbed him around the neck and held on. He chuckled. "Trust me. I'm not going to let you fall." He headed for the bedroom.

"Now to enjoy breakfast, the Aidan Westmoreland way," he said, easing her down on the bed. He stood back and stared at her for a long moment. "I want you so much I ache. I desire you so much I throb. And I will always love you, even after drawing my last breath."

For the second time that day, she fought back tears. "Oh, Aidan. I want, desire and love you, too. Just as much."

He leaned down and removed her shoes before removing every stitch of her clothing with a skill only he had perfected. When she lay there naked before him, he slid his pj's down his legs. "Lie still for a minute. There's something I want to do," he instructed in a throaty tone.

That's when Jillian saw the bottle of syrup he'd

brought into the bedroom with them. She looked at the bottle and then looked up at him. "You are kidding, right?"

"Do I look like I'm kidding?" he asked, removing the top.

She swallowed. No, he definitely didn't look as if he was kidding. In fact he looked totally serious. Too serious. "But I'm going to be all sticky," she reasoned. All she could think about was how glad she was for the bikini wax she'd gotten at the spa yesterday.

"You won't be sticky for long. I plan to lick it all off you and then we'll shower together."

"Aidan!" She squealed when she felt the thick liquid touch her skin. Aidan made good on his word. He dripped it all over her chest, making sure there was a lot covering her breasts, around her navel and lower still. He laid it on thick between her legs, drenching her womanly core.

And then he used his tongue to drive her insane with pleasure while taking his time to lick off all the syrup. The flick of his tongue sent sensuous shivers down her spine, and all she could do was lie there and moan while encased in a cloud of sensations.

He used his mouth as a bearer of pleasure as he laved her breasts, drawing the nipples between his lips and sucking on the turgid buds with a greed that made her womb contract. She wasn't sure how much more she could take when his mouth lowered to her stomach. She reached down and buried her fingers in his scalp as his mouth traced a hungry path around her navel.

Moments later he lifted his head to stare at her, deliberately licking his lips. They both knew where he was headed next. The look on his face said he wanted her to know he intended to go for the gusto.

And he did.

Jillian screamed his name the moment his tongue entered her, sending shockwaves of a gigantic orgasm through her body. His hot and greedy tongue had desire clawing at her insides, heightening her pulse. And when she felt another orgasm coming on the heels of the first, she knew it was time she took control. Otherwise, Aidan would lick her crazy.

With all the strength she could muster she tried to shift their bodies, which was hard to do since his mouth was on her while his hands held tight to her hips. When she saw there was no way she could make Aidan budge until he got his fill, she gave in to another scream when a second orgasm hit.

He finally lifted his head, smiled at her while licking his lips and then eased his body over hers. "I told you I was going to lick it all off you, baby."

Yes, he had. Then his engorged erection slid inside of her. All she recalled after that was her brain taking a holiday as passion overtook her, driving her over the edge, bringing her back, then driving her to the edge again.

He thrust hard, all the way to the hilt and then some. He lifted her hips and set the pace. The bed springs were tested to their maximum and so was she. She released a deep moan when he pounded into her, making her use muscles she hadn't used in a year. And then he slowed and without disconnecting their bodies, eased to his knees. He lifted her legs all the way to his shoulders and continued thrusting.

"Aidan!"

He answered with a deep growl when the same explosion that tore through her ripped through him, as well. She could feel his hot, molten liquid rush through her body, bathing her womb. But he didn't stop. He kept going, enlarging inside her all over again.

She saw arousal coiling in the depth of his eyes. They were in it for the long haul, right now and forever. And when his wet, slick body finally eased down, he pulled her into his arms, wrapped the strength of his legs over hers and held her close. She breathed in his scent. This was where she wanted to be. Always.

Hours later, Jillian stirred in Aidan's arms and eased over to whisper in his ear. "Remind me never to let you go without me for a full year again."

He grinned as he opened his eyes. "One year, two months and four days. But I wasn't counting or anything, mind you."

She smiled. "I'll take your word for it." She eased up to glance over at the clock. Had they been in bed five hours already? "We need to shower."

"Again?"

She laughed out. "The last time doesn't count."

"Why?"

She playfully glared over at him. "You know why."

He'd taken her into the shower to wash off any lingering stickiness from the syrup. Instead he ended up making love to her again. Then he'd dried them both off and had taken her to the bed and made love to her again several times, before they'd both drifted off to sleep.

"I guess we do need to get up, shower and dress if we want to see any of Monte Carlo."

"Yes, and I want to see Monte Carlo."

"I want to see you," he said, easing back and raking

his gaze over her naked body. "Do you know how much I missed this? Missed you?"

"The same way I missed you?"

"More," he said, running his hand over her body.

She couldn't ignore the delicious heat of the fingers touching her. "I doubt that, Dr. Westmoreland."

"Trust me."

She did trust him. And she loved him so much she wanted everyone to know it. "I can't wait until we return to Denver for Adrian's wedding."

He looked down at her. "Why?"

"So we can tell Pam and Dillon."

He studied her expression. "Are you ready for that?"

"More than ready. Do you think they already know?"

"It wouldn't surprise me if they did. Dillon isn't a dummy. Neither is Pam."

"Then why haven't they said anything?"

He shrugged. "Probably waiting for us to tell them."

She thought about what he'd said and figured he might be right. "Doesn't matter now. They will find out soon enough. Are you ready?"

"For another round?"

"No, not for another round. Are you ready to take a shower so we can get off this ship for a while?"

He pulled her into his arms. "Um, maybe. After another round." And then he lowered his mouth to hers.

Fourteen

"I hope you're not punishing me for what happened the last two days, Jillian."

Jillian glanced up at Aidan and smiled. "Why would I do that?" she asked as they walked the streets of Rome, Italy. She'd never visited a city more drenched in history. They would be here for two days and she doubted she could visit all the places she wanted to see in that time. She would have to make plans to come back one day.

"Because it was late when we finally got off the ship to tour Monte Carlo, and the same thing happened yesterday when we toured Florence. I have a feeling you blame me for both."

She chuckled. "Who else should I blame? Every time I mentioned it was time for us to get up, shower and get off the ship, you had other ideas."

He smiled as if remembering several of those ideas. "But we did do the tours. We just got a late start."

Yes, they had done the tours. For barely three hours in Monte Carlo. They had seen all they could in a cab ride around the city. Then yesterday, at least they had ridden up the most scenic road in Florence to reach Piazzale Michelangelo. From there they toured several palaces and museums before it was time to get back to the ship.

She had made sure they had gotten up, dressed and were off the ship at a reasonable time this morning for their tour of Rome. Already they had walked a lot, which was probably the reason Aidan was whining.

"What's the complaint, Aidan? You're in great shape." She of all people should know. He hadn't wasted time having her belongings moved into his suite where she had spent the night…and got very little sleep until dawn. But somehow she still felt energized.

"You think I'm punishing you by suggesting that we walk instead of taking a taxi-tour?" she asked as they crossed one of the busy streets.

"No. I think you're punishing me because you talked me out of renting that red Ferrari. Just think of all the places I could have taken you while driving it."

She chuckled. "Yes, but I would have wanted to get there in one piece and without an accelerated heart rate."

He placed his arms around her shoulders. "Have you forgotten that one day I intend to be one of the most sought-after cardiologists in the world?"

"How could I forget?" she said, smiling. She was really proud of him and his accomplishments. Going through that dual residency program was what had opened the door for him to continue his specialty training at Johns Hopkins, one of the most renowned research hospitals in the country.

Last night, in between making love, they had talked about their future goals. He knew she would start her residency at a hospital in Orlando, Florida, in the fall. The good thing was that after a year of internship, she could transfer to another hospital. Because he would be working for at least three years at John Hopkins, she would try to relocate to the Washington, D.C., or Maryland area.

A few hours later they had toured a number of places, including the Colosseum, St. Peter's Basilica, the Trevi Fountain and the Catacombs. While standing in front of the Spanish Steps, waiting for Aidan to return from retrieving the lace fan she'd left behind in the church of Trinità dei Monti, she blinked when she saw a familiar man pass by.

Riley Westmoreland? What was Aidan's cousin doing in Rome?

"Riley!" she yelled out. When the man didn't look her way, she figured he must not have heard her. Taking the steps almost two at a time, she hurriedly raced after him.

When she caught up with him she grabbed his arm. "Riley, wait up! I didn't know you—"

She stopped in midsentence when the man turned around. It wasn't Riley. But he looked enough like him to be a twin. "I'm so sorry. I thought you were someone else."

The man smiled and she blinked. He even had Riley's smile. Or more specifically, one of those Westmoreland smiles. All the men in the family had dimples. And like all the Westmoreland men, he was extremely handsome.

"No problem, signorina."

She smiled. "You're Italian?" she asked.

"No. American. I'm here on business. And you?"

"American. Here vacationing." She extended her hand. "I'm Jillian Novak."

He nodded as he took her hand. "Garth Outlaw."

"Nice meeting you, Garth, and again I'm sorry that I mistook you for someone else, but you and Riley Westmoreland could almost be twins."

He chuckled. "A woman as beautiful as you can do whatever you like, signorina. No need to apologize." He grasped her hand and lifted it to his lips. "Have a good day, beautiful Jillian Novak, and enjoy the rest of your time in Rome."

"And you do the same."

He turned and walked away. She stood there for a minute, thinking. He was even a flirt like those Westmorelands before they'd married. And the man even had that Westmoreland sexy walk. How crazy was that?

"Jillian?" She turned when she heard Aidan call her name.

"I thought you were going to wait for me on the steps," he said when he reached her.

"I did but then I thought I saw Riley and—"

"Riley? Trust me, Riley would not be in Rome, especially not with Alpha expecting their baby any day now."

"I know, but this guy looked so much like Riley that I raced after him. He could have been Riley's twin. I apologized for my mistake and he was nice about it. He was an American, here on business. Said his name was Garth Outlaw. And he really did favor Riley."

Aidan frowned. "Outlaw?"

"Yes."

"Um, that's interesting. The last time we had our family meeting about the investigation Rico is handling, I think he said something about tracing a branch of the Westmoreland roots to a family who goes by the last name of Outlaw."

"Really?"

"That's what I recall, but Dillon would know for sure. I'll mention it to him when we return home. That information might help Rico," Aidan said as they walked back toward the Spanish Steps.

Rico Claiborne, a private investigator, was married

to Aidan's sister Megan. Jillian was aware that Rico's PI firm had been investigating the connection of four women to Aidan's great-grandfather, Raphel Westmoreland. It had been discovered during a genealogy search that before marrying Aidan's great-grandmother Gemma, Raphel had been connected to four other women who'd been listed as former wives. Rico's investigation had confirmed that Raphel hadn't married any of the women, but that one of them had given birth to a son that Raphel had never known about. Evidently, Jillian thought, at some point Rico had traced that son to the Outlaw family.

"Ready to head back to the ship?" Aidan asked, interrupting her thoughts.

She glanced back at her watch. "Yes, it's getting kind of late. You can join me and the book-club ladies when we go shopping tomorrow if you'd like."

He shook his head. "No thanks. Although it's a beautiful city, I've seen enough of Rome for now. But I will bring you back."

She lifted a brow. "You will?"

"Yes."

"When?"

"For our honeymoon. I hope." Aidan then got down on one knee and took her hand in his. "I love you, Jillian. Will you marry me?"

Jillian stared at him in shock. It was only when he tugged at her hand did she notice the ring he'd placed there. Her eyes widened. "Oh, my God!" Never had she seen anything so beautiful.

"Well?" Aidan asked, grinning. "People are standing around. We've gotten their attention. Are you going to embarrass me or what?"

She saw that people had stopped to stare. They had heard his proposal and, like Aidan, they were waiting for her answer. She could not believe that here in the beautiful city of Rome, on the Spanish Steps, Aidan had asked her to marry him. She would remember this day for as long as she lived.

"Yes. Yes!" she said, filled with happiness. "Yes, I will marry you."

"Thank you," he said, getting back to his feet and pulling her into his arms. "For a minute there you had me worried."

The people around them cheered and clapped while a smiling Aidan pulled Jillian into his arms and kissed her.

Aidan walked down the long corridor to his suite. Jillian had sent him away an hour ago with instructions not to return until now because she would have a surprise waiting for him when he got back. He smiled thinking she had probably planned a candlelit dinner for their last day on the cruise.

It was hard to believe their two weeks were up. Tomorrow they would return to Barcelona. After two days in Rome they had spent two days at sea before touring Athens, Greece. While there they had taken part in a wine-tasting excursion and visited several museums. From there they had toured Turkey, Mykonos and Malta. Now they were headed back to Barcelona and would arrive before daybreak.

He couldn't help the feeling of happiness that puffed out his chest when he thought of being an engaged man. Although they hadn't set a date, the most important thing was that he had asked and she had said yes. They talked every day about their future, and although they still had at least another year before she could join him in Maryland, they were okay with it because they knew the day would come when they would be together.

They decided not to wait until they went home for Adrian's wedding to tell the family their news. Some would be shocked, while others who knew about their affair would be relieved that their secret wasn't a secret any longer. They would head straight to Denver tomorrow when the ship docked.

He chuckled when he thought about Jillian's excitement over her engagement ring. The book-club ladies had definitely been impressed as well, ahhing and ooing every night at dinner. Jewelry by Zion was the rave since Zion was the First Lady's personal jeweler. Jillian hadn't known that he knew Zion personally because of Aidan's friendship with the Steele family, who were close personal friends of Zion. Zion had designed most of his signature custom jewelry collection while living in Rome for the past ten years. Thanks to Dominic, Aidan had met with Zion privately on board the ship in the wee hours of the morning while Jillian slept, when they first docked in a port near Rome. Zion had brought an attaché case filled with beautiful rings—all originals hand-crafted by Zion. When Aidan had seen this one particular ring, he'd known it was the one he wanted to put on Jillian's finger.

When Aidan reached his suite's door, he knocked, to let her know he had returned.

"Come in."

Using his passkey, he opened the door and smiled upon seeing the lit candles around the room. His bride-to-be had set the mood for a romantic dinner, he thought, when he saw how beautifully the table was set.

Closing the door behind him he glanced around the dimly lit suite but didn't see Jillian anywhere. Was she in the bedroom waiting on him? He moved in that direction and then felt a hand on his shoulder. He turned around and his breath caught. Jillian wore a provocative black lace teddy that showed a lot of flesh. Attached to the teddy were matching lace garters and she wore a pair of stilettoes on her feet. He thought he hadn't seen anyone as sexy in his entire life and he couldn't help groaning in appreciation.

She leaned close, swirled the tip of her tongue around his ear and whispered, "I'm about to give you the lap dance of your life, Aidan Westmoreland."

The next thing he knew he was gently shoved in a chair. "And remember no touching, so put your hands behind your back."

He followed her instructions, mesmerized beyond belief. Her sensual persona stirred his desire. His pulse kicked up a notch, followed immediately by a deep throbbing in his erection. "And just what do you want me to do?" he asked in a low voice.

She smiled at him. "Just enjoy. I plan to do all the work. But by the time I finish, you will be too exhausted to move."

Really? Him? Too exhausted to move? And she would be the one doing all the work? He couldn't wait for that experience. "Now will you keep your hands to yourself or do I need to handcuff you?" she asked him.

He couldn't help smiling at the thought of that. Did she really have handcuffs? Would she be that daring? He decided to find out. "I can't make any promises, so you might want to handcuff me."

"No problem."

The next thing he knew she'd whipped out a pair of handcuffs slapped them on his wrists and locked them with a click to the chair. *Damn.* While he was taking all this in, he suddenly heard music coming from the sound system in the room. He didn't recognize the artist, but the song had a sensual beat.

While sitting there handcuffed to the chair, he watched as Jillian responded to the music, her movements slow, graceful and seductive. She rolled her stomach and then shimmied her hips and backside in a sinfully erotic way. He sat there awestruck, fascinated, staring at her as she moved in front of him. He felt the rapid beat of his heart and the sweet pull of desire as his erection continued to pulsate.

Although he couldn't touch her, she was definitely touching him—rubbing her hands over his shirt, underneath it, through the hair on his chest, before taking her time unbuttoning his shirt and easing it from his shoulders.

"Have I ever told you how much I love your chest, Aidan?" she asked him in a sultry tone.

"No," he answered huskily. "You never have."

"Well, I'm telling you now. In fact, I want to show you just how much I like it."

Then she crouched over him and used her tongue to lick his shoulder blades before moving slowly across the span of his chest. He would have come out of his chair had he not been handcuffed to it. She used her tongue in ways she hadn't before and he heard himself groaning out loud.

"You like that?" she asked, leaning close to his mouth, and licking there, as well. "Want more? Want to see what else you've taught me to do with my tongue?"

He swallowed. Oh, yes, he wanted more. He wanted to see just what he'd taught her. Instead of answering, he nodded.

She smiled as she bent down to remove his shoes. Reaching up, she unzipped his pants and he raised his hips as she slid both his pants and briefs down his legs. She smiled at him again.

"You once licked me all over, Aidan, and you seemed to have enjoyed it. Now I'm going to do the same to you and I intend to enjoy myself, as well."

Moistening her lips with a delicious-looking sweep of her tongue, she got down on her knees before him and spread his legs. Then she lowered her head between his thighs and took him into her mouth.

As soon as she touched him, blood rushed through his veins, sexual hunger curled his stomach and desire stroked his gut. Her mouth widened to accommodate his size and she used her tongue to show that with this, she was definitely in control. He watched in a sensual daze as her head bobbed up and down while she fanned the blaze of his desire.

He wanted to grab hold of her hair, stroke her back, caress her shoulders but he couldn't. He felt defenseless, totally under her control but he loved every single minute of it. When he couldn't take any more, his body jerked in one hell of an explosion and she still wouldn't let go.

"Jillian!"

He wanted her with an intensity that terrified him. And when she lifted her head and smiled at him, he knew what it meant to love someone with every part of your heart, your entire being and your soul.

While the music continued to play, she straightened and began stripping for him, removing each piece of clothing slowly, and teasing his nostrils before tossing it aside. Sexual excitement filled his inner core as he inhaled her scent. When she was totally naked, she began dancing again, touching herself and touching him. He'd never seen anything so erotic in his entire life.

When she curled into his lap and continued to dance, the feel of her soft curves had him growling, had his erection throbbing again, harder. "Set me free," he begged. He needed to touch her now. He wanted his hands in her hair and his fingers inside her.

"Not yet," she whispered in a purr that made even more need wash over him. Then she twisted her body around so her back was plastered to his chest then she eased down onto his manhood and rode him.

Never had she ridden him this hard and when she shifted so they faced each other, the feel of her breasts hitting his chest sent all kinds of sensations through him.

"Jillian!"

He screamed her name as an orgasm hit him again, deep, and he pulled the scent of her sex through his nostrils. He leaned forward. Although he couldn't touch her, he could lick her. He used his tongue to touch her earlobe and her face. "Uncuff me baby. Please. Uncuff me now."

She reached behind him and he heard the click that released him. When his hands were free he stood, with her in his arms, and quickly moved toward the bedroom.

"You're the one who was supposed to be exhausted," she mumbled into his chest.

"Sorry, it doesn't quite work that way, baby." And then he stretched her out on the bed.

He straddled her, eased inside her and thrust, stroking her, wanting her to feel his love in every movement. This was erotic pleasure beyond compare and her inner muscles clenched him, held him tight and tempted him to beg again.

His thrusts became harder, her moans louder and the desire he felt for her more relentless than ever. And when he finally exploded, he took her along with him as an earth-shattering climax claimed them both. They were blasted into the heavens. Jillian Novak had delivered the kind of mindless pleasure every man should experience at least once in his lifetime. And he was glad that he had.

Moments later, he eased off her and pulled her into his arms, entwining her legs with his. He kissed the side of her face while she fell into a deep sleep.

Their secret affair was not a secret any longer and he couldn't wait to tell the world that he'd found his mate for life. And he would cherish her forever.

Epilogue

"So, you thought you were keeping a secret from us," Pam said, smiling, sitting beside her husband on the sofa as they met with Aidan and Jillian.

"But we didn't?" Jillian asked, grinning and holding Aidan's hand.

"For a little while, maybe," Dillon replied. But when you fall in love with someone, it's hard to keep something like that hidden, especially in *this* family."

Jillian knew exactly what Dillon meant. It seemed the bigger secret had been that she and Aidan had wanted to keep their relationship a secret. No one in the family knew who else knew, so everyone kept their suspicions to themselves.

"Well, I'm glad we don't have to hide things anymore," Aidan said, standing, pulling Jillian up with him and then wrapping his arms around her shoulders.

"You mean you don't have to *try* and hide things," Pam corrected. "Neither of you were doing such a good job of pretending. And when the two of you had that rift, Dillon and I were tempted to intervene. But we figured if it was meant for the two of you to be together, you would be, without our help."

Jillian looked down at her ring. "Yes, we were able to get our act together, although I will have to give Paige some credit for bailing out of the cruise. Aidan and I needed that time together to work things out."

"And I guess from that ring on your finger, the two of you managed to do that," Dillon said.

Aidan nodded as he smiled down at Jillian. "Yes, we did. The thought of a year-long engagement doesn't bother us. After Jillian's first year at that hospital in Orlando, Florida, she'll be able to transfer to one near me. That's when we plan to tie the knot."

"Besides," Pam said, smiling. "The year gives me plenty of time to plan for the wedding without feeling rushed. These Westmoreland weddings are coming around fast, but trust me, I'm not complaining."

Dillon reached out and hugged his wife. "Please don't complain. I'm elated with each one. After Adrian gets hitched next month and Aidan is married in a year, all we'll have to be concerned with is Bailey and Bane."

The room got quiet as everyone thought about that. Only two Westmorelands were left single, and those two were known to be the most headstrong of them all.

"Bay says she's never getting married," Aidan said, grinning.

"So did you and Adrian," Dillon reminded him. "In fact, I don't think there's a single Westmoreland who hasn't made that claim at some point in time, including me. But all it takes is for one of us to find that special person who's our soul mate, and we start singing a different tune."

"But can you see Bay singing a different tune?" Aidan asked.

Dillon thought about the question for a minute, drew in a deep breath and then shook his head. "No."

Everyone laughed. When their laughter subsided Pam smiled and said, "There's someone for everyone, including Bailey. She just hasn't met him yet. In other words, Bailey hasn't met her match. But one day, I believe that she will."

The following month

"Adrian Westmoreland, you may kiss your bride."

Aidan, serving as best man, smiled as he watched his twin brother take the woman he loved, Dr. Trinity Matthews Westmoreland, into his arms to seal their marriage vows with one hell of a kiss. Aidan spotted Jillian in the audience sitting with her sisters and winked at her. Their day would be coming and he couldn't wait.

A short while later, Aidan stole his twin away for a few minutes. The wedding had been held in Trinity's hometown of Bunnell, Florida, at the same church where their cousin Thorn had married Trinity's sister Tara. The weather had been beautiful and it seemed everyone in the little town had been invited to the wedding, which accounted for the packed church of more than eight hundred guests. The reception was held in the ballroom of a beautiful hotel overlooking the Atlantic Ocean.

"Great job, Dr. Westmoreland," he said, grinning at Adrian.

Adrian chuckled. "I intend to say the same to you

a year from now, Dr. Westmoreland, when you tie the knot. I'm glad the cruise helped, and that you and Jillian were able to work things out."

"So am I. That had to be the worst year of my life when we were apart."

Adrian nodded. "I know. Remember I felt your pain whenever you let out any strong emotions."

Yes, Aidan did remember. "So where are you headed for your honeymoon?"

"Sydney, Australia. I've always wanted to go back, and I look forward to taking Trinity there with me."

"Well, the two of you deserve a lifetime of happiness," Aidan said, taking a sip of his champagne.

"You and Jillian do, as well. I'm so glad the secret is a secret no longer."

Aidan's smile widened. "So am I. And on that note, I'm going to go claim my fiancée so you can go claim your bride."

Aidan crossed the span of the ball room to where Jillian stood with her sisters Paige and Nadia, and his sister Bailey. He and Jillian would leave Bunnell in the morning and take the hour-long drive to Orlando. Together they would look for an apartment for her close to the hospital where she would be working as an intern. He had checked and discovered that flights from the D.C. area into Orlando were pretty frequent. He was glad about that because he intended to pay his woman plenty of visits.

Aidan had told Dillon about Jillian's chance meeting with a man by the name of Garth Outlaw while in Rome and how she'd originally thought he was Riley.

Dillon wasn't surprised that any kin out there would have the Westmoreland look due to dominant genes. He had passed the information on to Rico. The family was hoping something resulted from Jillian's encounter.

"Sorry, ladies, I need to grab Jillian for a minute," he said, snagging her hand.

"Where are we going?" Jillian asked as he led her toward the exit.

"To walk on the beach."

"Okay."

Holding hands, they crossed the boardwalk and went down the steps. Pausing briefly, they removed their shoes. Jillian moaned when her feet touched the sand.

"What are you thinking about, baby?" Aidan asked her.

"I'm thinking about how wonderful I feel right now. Walking in the sand, being around the people I love, not having to hide my feelings for you. And what a lucky woman I am to have such a loving family and such a gorgeous and loving fiancé."

He glanced down at her. "You think I'm gorgeous?"

"Yes."

"You think I'm loving?"

"Definitely."

"Will that qualify me for another lap dance tonight?"

Jillian threw her head back and laughed, causing the wind to send hair flying across her face. Aidan pushed her hair back and she smiled up at him.

"Dr. Westmoreland, you can get a lap dance out of me anytime. Just say the word."

"Lap dance."

She leaned up on tip toes. "You got it."

Aidan then pulled her into his arms and kissed her. Life couldn't get any better than this.

* * * * *

If you loved Aidan, pick up his twin's story,
THE REAL THING
by New York Times *and* USA TODAY
bestselling author Brenda Jackson.
Available now, from Harlequin Desire!

REQUEST YOUR FREE BOOKS!
2 FREE NOVELS PLUS 2 FREE GIFTS!

HARLEQUIN®

Desire

ALWAYS POWERFUL, PASSIONATE AND PROVOCATIVE

YES! Please send me 2 FREE Harlequin Desire® novels and my 2 FREE gifts (gifts are worth about $10). After receiving them, if I don't wish to receive any more books, I can return the shipping statement marked "cancel." If I don't cancel, I will receive 6 brand-new novels every month and be billed just $4.55 per book in the U.S. or $4.99 per book in Canada. That's a savings of at least 13% off the cover price! It's quite a bargain! Shipping and handling is just 50¢ per book in the U.S. and 75¢ per book in Canada.* I understand that accepting the 2 free books and gifts places me under no obligation to buy anything. I can always return a shipment and cancel at any time. Even if I never buy another book, the two free books and gifts are mine to keep forever.

225/326 HDN F4ZC

Name _____ (PLEASE PRINT)

Address _____ Apt. #

City _____ State/Prov. _____ Zip/Postal Code

Signature (if under 18, a parent or guardian must sign)

Mail to the **Harlequin® Reader Service:**
IN U.S.A.: P.O. Box 1867, Buffalo, NY 14240-1867
IN CANADA: P.O. Box 609, Fort Erie, Ontario L2A 5X3

Want to try two free books from another line?
Call 1-800-873-8635 or visit www.ReaderService.com.

* Terms and prices subject to change without notice. Prices do not include applicable taxes. Sales tax applicable in N.Y. Canadian residents will be charged applicable taxes. Offer not valid in Quebec. This offer is limited to one order per household. Not valid for current subscribers to Harlequin Desire books. All orders subject to credit approval. Credit or debit balances in a customer's account(s) may be offset by any other outstanding balance owed by or to the customer. Please allow 4 to 6 weeks for delivery. Offer available while quantities last.

Your Privacy—The Harlequin® Reader Service is committed to protecting your privacy. Our Privacy Policy is available online at www.ReaderService.com or upon request from the Harlequin Reader Service.

We make a portion of our mailing list available to reputable third parties that offer products we believe may interest you. If you prefer that we not exchange your name with third parties, or if you wish to clarify or modify your communication preferences, please visit us at www.ReaderService.com/consumerschoice or write to us at Harlequin Reader Service Preference Service, P.O. Box 9062, Buffalo, NY 14269. Include your complete name and address.

HD13R

SPECIAL EXCERPT FROM

 HARLEQUIN®

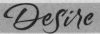 *Desire*

Here's an exciting sneak preview of
Cat Schield's
BECAUSE OF THE BABY...

As *TEXAS CATTLEMAN'S CLUB: AFTER THE STORM*
continues, two members of feuding families come together
to care for a very special baby born during the tornado...

"It would be better for you if I was here full-time," Keaton said.

"How do you figure?"

"Have you considered what will happen if Grace is up all night? If I'm here we can take turns getting up with her." He could see Lark was weakening. "It makes sense."

"Let me sleep on it tonight?" She held out her hands for the baby.

"Sure."

Only, Lark never got the chance to sleep. Neither did Keaton. Shortly after Grace finished eating, she began to fuss. During the second hour of the baby's crying, Keaton searched for advice on his tablet.

"She's dry, fed and obviously tired. Why won't she sleep?"

"Because it's her first day out of the NICU and she's overstimulated."

"How about wrapping her up?" he suggested. "Says here that babies feel more secure when they're swaddled." He cued up a video and they watched it. The demonstration looked straightforward, but the woman in the video used a doll, not a real baby.

"We can try it." Lark went to the closet and returned with two blankets of different sizes. "Hopefully one of these will do the trick."

When she was done, Lark braced her hands on the dining room table and stared down at the swaddled baby. "This doesn't look right."

Keaton returned to the video. "I think we missed this part here."

Grace was growing more upset by the second and she'd managed to free her left arm.

"Is it terrible that I have no idea what I'm doing?" Lark sounded close to tears. It had been a long, stressful evening.

"Not at all. I think every first-time parent feels just as overwhelmed as we do right now."

"Thank you for sticking around and helping me."

"We're helping Grace."

The corners of her lips quivered. "Not very well, as it happens."

And then, because she looked determined and hopeless all at once, Keaton succumbed to the impulse that had been threatening to break free all week. He cupped her cheek, lowered his head and kissed her.

Don't miss BECAUSE OF THE BABY...
by Cat Schield
Available January 2015
wherever Harlequin® Desire books and ebooks are sold.

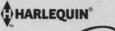

HARLEQUIN®

Desire

ALWAYS POWERFUL, PASSIONATE AND PROVOCATIVE.

SNOWED IN WITH HER EX
by **Andrea Laurence**

Available January 2015

**Trapped in a cabin with the man who makes
her want what she shouldn't have…**

Wedding photographer Briana Harper never
expected to run into her ex at an engagement shoot!
And when a blizzard strands them…alone…in a
remote mountain cabin, she knows she's in trouble.
She's never forgotten Ian Lawson, but none of the reasons
they broke up have changed. He's still a workaholic.
And now he's an *engaged* workaholic!

But Ian is also still a man who knows what he wants.
And what he wants is Briana. Untangling the lies of his
current engagement leaves him free to…indulge.
Yet proving he's changed may be this music mogul's
toughest negotiation yet…

SNOWED IN WITH HER EX
is the first installment in **Andrea Laurence's**
Brides and Belles series:

~ Wedding planning is their business…and their pleasure ~

Available wherever Harlequin® *Desire
books and ebooks are sold.*

HD73362